Richard J Price was born in 1966. He grew up in Renfrewshire and was educated at Napier College and the University of Strathclyde. He has a doctorate from Strathclyde for his study of Neil Gunn's fiction and drama. Critic, editor and poet, his books include *The Fabulous Matter of Fact: the Poetics of Neil M Gunn* and the pamphlet collections *Marks and Sparks, Tube Shelter Perspective, Sense and a Minor Fever*, and *Hand Held*.

He collaborated with the artist-printer Ron King to produce the artist's book *gift horse* (Circle Press, 1999), and with fellow poet Raymond Friel to produce the collection *Renfrewshire in Old Photographs*. His first full-length poetry book, *Perfume and Petrol Fumes*, was published by Diehard in 1999, followed by *Frosted, Melted* in 2002.

Price has been an editor of several influential poetry magazines: *Gairfish, Verse, Southfields*, and the current *Painted, spoken*; he is also co-founder of Vennel Press, a small press that was responsible for the early publications of poets W N Herbert, David Kinloch, Elizabeth James, and Peter McCarey.

Other publications include *Contraflow on the Superhighway* (an anthology of Informationist poetry, co-edited with W N Herbert), *Eftirs/ Afters* (translations of French modernist lyric poets, with Donny O'Rourke), *César Vallejo* (co-edited with Stephen Watts), *La nouvelle alliance* (essays on French influences on Scottish literature, co-edited with David Kinloch) and *The star you steer by* (essays on the English modernist Basil Bunting, co-edited with James McGonigal).

Richard J Price is Curator of Modern British Collections at the British Library, London. He is married with two children. *A Boy in Summer* is his first collection of short stories.

There's a point where you can see a supersonic jet and it's totally silent before the sound crashes in, a pause before you realise the force and energy. Reading Richard Price is like that moment. This man is headed for the future.

S B Kelly, *The Eildon Tree*

A lyrical collection which explores family and memory. Price's imagery is electric, with a capacity to integrate phrases from supposedly non-poetic sources to great effect... It is a *tour-de-force*; encompassing raw honesty and the most tender of paternal love poems.

S B Kelly on *Frosted, Melted, Scotland on Sunday*

Versatile and challenging... this is poetry with its pulse on the times and its perspective is international. Price can be hard-edged, modernist, lyrical, even downright sentimental. Constants in his work are extreme economy and a lively wit, beyond that the world is his subject, but very much the modern world with its fleeting impressions, fetishes, sexuality, and vulnerability... His voice is alive and burning with purpose.

John Hudson, *Markings*

Richard Price has for more than a decade been writing some of the tautest, tenderest, shearest and most beguilingly distinctive poetry to have appeared in this country. That it has taken until now for a substantial collection of his poems to find a publisher baffles ... His work ... can be pregnantly elliptical and resonantly opaque in places, it is true (leaving the reader to do a little work!) but which for the most part sings with a gorgeous and pellucid simplicity that makes him an extremely accessible and engaging writer. What a gathering of gifts this elegantly crammed wee book represents.

Donny O'Rourke, *Herald*

www.11-9.co.uk

A Boy in Summer
Short Stories
R J Price

First published by

303a The Pentagon Centre
36 Washington Street
GLASGOW
G3 8AZ

Tel: 0141 204 1109
Fax: 0141 221 5363

E-mail: info@nwp.sol.co.uk
www.11-9.co.uk

A catalogue record for this book is available from the British Library

11:9 is funded by the Scottish Arts
Council National Lottery Fund

ISBN 1 903238 50 1

Typeset in Utopia
11:9 series designed by Mark Blackadder

Printed in Finland by WS Bookwell

Acknowledgements
Many of these short stories first appeared in
Southfields, in *The Eildon Tree*, and in *Ape*

For my father,
and for Tim, Dave, and Rob,
and in memory of my mother.

Contents

Go with the boy from the business park.
That's the future, I'm sure you're right.
Take your creams and your credit cards
and meet that boy tonight.

1

A Car Park

Between the gravel floor of the pub's car park and the clear night sky was a bubble of life – drinkers walking to their cars.

The scent of perhaps only six or seven brands of perfume was behind as many as thirty pairs of ears, and the men's aftershave was reciprocating. The mingled fragrances were made gentle in the open. There was banter between men and women, between women and women, men and men. In the moving crowd everyone's smoky hair and hot but cooling skin was infusing everything with a kind of sensual good nature.

Some cars were already leaving. They were being carefully navigated through the couples and little groups, a driver here and there winding down his window to speak to a friend he or she had neglected earlier. 'We'll be at the Grist on Friday!' 'I saw your wee sister earlier – said she was going up to a club.' 'Aye, engaged! About time, as well!' Then a toot on the horn and cars were leaving completely.

Some were very full. In fact there was a local tradition, when needs must, of carrying folk back in the boot. Last autumn there had been an accident when a booter had got a scare and a broken collarbone. Despite some of the vehicles groaning on their axles there was none quite so packed tonight.

Many of the drivers had been trying not to drink all evening but most had had one or two. One man, whose count must have been nearer double figures, had begun casual-like to search his pockets for his car keys. Now he was getting het up standing by his car, a sporty special. In this light the car looked grey-y yellow. He was going through the third repeat of what he no doubt considered a logical sequence: top left outside pocket, top left inside, bottom left... It did not help that he had one of those rural-type oiled coats which have so many hiding places, some resistant to even clear-headed reasoning. Arranged in almost a line on the car roof were his paunched wallet, some worn tissues, a boiled sweet, and a pile of small brown change; he seemed to be talking to them. Already he was being theatrically pitied as people went by. 'That's a sin!' 'Aw, look at that guy!'...

The people who had been in small groups inside shouted the ends of their conversations as they walked to their own cars. Couples found their own more intimate company ready for less public talk, and lowered their voices.

A few particularly young-looking men appeared the most sober of all the crowd. Each an owner of a new driving licence, they had been acting as taxi-drivers for their elder siblings, so they could get use of the family car. They had not been drinking, and now couldn't conceal their disappointment. Each felt that all evening his elder had been holding off from initiating him into the young adult world, that perhaps it was only alcohol itself that could do that, and now they were being treated like mere chauffeurs. The extraordinary good nature of the tipping-out was lost on them.

Some people were helping drivers to back out of tough parking spaces. Apart from the wall of the Fox and Hounds itself, the rectangular car park was bound on two sides by a stout wall naturally camouflaged with the colour of rock and lichen. At the back the gravel thinned into rough grass (where a number of 'overflow' cars had been parked) and beyond that there was a dark unfenced burn. As well as these hazards there were other cars to consider and some had been parked very individualistically.

When the car park had half-emptied, which happened within a couple of minutes, the problem subsided and the semaphore merchants were needed less. The noise and the scent had begun to dissolve and as you could hear the burn again so you could sense the coarse grasses in late flower, the cooling dust and the stones of the gravel, that clear air. The voices of those who lived locally could be heard, too, as they walked home.

At last, all that was in the car park was a single, sporty, car.

In the morning its colour, red, would return, and so would its driver.

The Mill Pool

When the lawns hardened in the week or two of high summer, children and teenagers would meet up round the rim of a little artificial loch. They'd come, juice-bottles in hand, from the new private houses nearby, from the tenements over the shops, and from the scheme on the other side of the village. This was the Mill Pool.

The building at the water's edge didn't seem much of a mill: there was no wheel. It was like a big red barn with corrugated sides; a corrugated roof, too; factory-like, as if it had been stapled together. Everyone knew the building was just used for 'storage', but no one knew for what.

The water didn't seem dangerous, not like the weir-pools

in the next village downstream. Over the years, perhaps a dozen lives had been lost in those, in one incident a father trying to rescue his drowning son. The river had got muscle on its shanks by then.

Roughly speaking, secondary school kids swam in the mill pool, primary school kids paddled. If you had a snorkeller's mask, and some did, you could see large lithe brown trout clearly ahead of you. They moved at just more than arm's length, as alive as the children clocking them. If the fish were untouchable here, they could soon enough be guddled by a trained hand downstream. But that *would* be training. Choosing the boulder whose earthy shadow they were biding in, and having the hand to stroke them out: these were skills to be coveted.

A boxy tranny would be quietly on, standing on one of the sandy-coloured blocks of stone that lay round the edge nearest the tractor track. The other side of the pool had a thin stand of small trees, birches maybe, and hawthorns, but was cut off by leaf-matted netting which went right across the stretch of water, just keeking above it. Where this flexed fence came out either side it was a good seven feet high and secured by tilted stanchions bolted into concrete. Though you might not know it (though everyone did), the river-proper was beyond the other side of the trees. The pool was fed by the millrace, or lade, that drew from much further upstream. The lade rejoined the river soon after the mill, just before a road bridge, but the confluence was not turbulent. It must once have been. Beyond the trees you could see pasture gently rising to Balcraigie, an off-white building with a single stout castellated tower. It looked slightly off balance. Built at the end of Queen Victoria's reign as a home for orphans of sailors, it had since been a school for young offenders. Though now a private house, the parental threat, 'I'll send ye to Balcraigie,' was still viable.

At the Mill Pool most of the kids would be in T-shirts and shorts (sometimes just old denims cut down to the knees). Some teenage boys, who said shorts were for weans, always wore full-length jeans and just sat in small mannish groups by the waterside. They might play ponnies or five-stanes. The swimmers would have a towel rolled up with their swimming costume in it. No one noticed that boys called it their 'trunks', but girls called theirs a 'cozzie' or a 'swimsuit'.

Usually you would use a towel to change behind, but that was in the daytime. Those in their late teens would be around until ten or eleven if the evening was a clear one, and then they might not observe all the niceties. That meant there'd be a laugh about the nudity, a sprint into the covering water, waist-high for men, shoulders for the lassies, and then a sprint out again and into clothes. It would be a bet or just a joke.

That late, one of the oldest lads might have scored some Lebanese from a pub in the Port or the Brig, or brought some grass grown quietly among tomatoes and peppers in their parents' conservatory, in a sky-lit attic, or on a high dripping windowsill. There'd be a low continuous bubbling of laughter on those evenings, a kind of human echoing of the old lade and of the river itself. The young women and their men would play children's games like tig and count one hundred, enjoy the rushing and grabbing, and most would go no further than the public kind of kissing that said, yes, we're together. If there were more to it, it would be in private, later.

A Group Arrest

The boy who'd rolled his mother's car, winning the race on the airport boundary road, travelled back in the boot of his mate's dad's BMW. Alive, just scratched.

This meant the losing car's passenger list doubled. In the front, driving, Lord Jamie. Keeping him company, Frank, Julie and Ross. In the back: Swedger, Tom, Sylvia, Alison, Callum, and Sheila. And someone whose name I always forget, from Bishopton.

The boot, as I said, had Michael, but also Anne-Marie Johnson-Nardini (her mother said to her boyfriends her name was longer than she was). Her nickname was Cappuccino.

Jamie reckoned the police would be sitting, set back a little, at the bypass junction next to Kilpeter Catholic Primary. So he took the country road past the quarry and the Ordnance Factory, doubling back straight through the village. All going well he'd give the police the slip by exiting via South Mound and so on to Bridge of Weir.

This worked fine until the car came into Kilpeter on the War Memorial road. The idea being 'softly, softly', the literalist Jamie put it into neutral at the crown of the hill, killed the beams, and turned the engine off. The car began rolling down the steep High Street, silent as planned.

But as the car passed the Kilpeter Inn, Jamie shouted, as if spontaneously, 'The Kil-peee-terrr Inn!' Everyone knew there and then he'd just invented a new game, including Michael and Cappuccino in the boot, who were thankful for something to break the ice. When the car reached the next pub, they all joined in: 'The C-er-ross Keeeeee-ys!'.

They then breathed in for the last and poshest hostelry at the foot of the brae.

It turned out, though, that the police had just cleared up a small misunderstanding there, and PC Edwards and WPC Edwards (no relation) were at that moment giving way at the exit of the car park, Alec Ramsay looking sheepish in the back. They three saw the whole thing, which was a low-on-its-axles executive company car zooming down towards them, sans lights, and no sound of a zoom. And, as the black BMW passed their striped Mini Metro all they could hear, with a volume that suggested the car itself was alive, was: 'The Fo-o-o-o-o-x and Hou-ow-ow-ow-nds!'

2

Roughcast

Lawrence Ford hired a car at Renfrew Airport and drove out towards the village of Kilellan.

He knew he had lost his way when he passed the large factory that was the home, the billboards said, of the Hillman Imp. This was several miles off course.

There were large numbers of council houses, many clad in the grey and sandy roughcast of the Scottish vernacular. These were the kinds of houses he would be helping to construct elsewhere now that he was the Contracts Manager for the Build Scotland Association.

Did the householders actually like roughcast? Since he

had accepted the job, he had seen no comment from residents or residents' groups. None of the pre-specification documents mentioned the residents' points of view.

Normally, this would not have struck Ford as odd. He'd been involved in the construction of many hospitals and libraries, and patients and readers were not usually asked their opinions directly. The grubby quartz walls of these houses seemed so unappealing, though, that he wondered if consultation would not have been wise. He found the look of these buildings immediately depressing.

Perhaps an issue like traditional roughcast was not controversial in Scotland. Ford was glad he had become disorientated. He might not have had the chance to see such large tracts of housing if he had kept to the Association's directions. It was always better to know more than your employer thought you knew. The brochures, albeit for the new projects, bore little resemblance to what he was seeing now. Of course, artist's impressions always made homes out of holes and ghosts out of residents. As he was also choosing a home for his own family, he had especially to bear that in mind.

He soon found his way back on to the Kilellan road, and entered the village only a few minutes later than planned.

He drove up the steep hill to the towering Hydro Hotel and parked his car close to the entrance. This was a building that was more his style. It reminded him of some of the old spacious apartment blocks he'd seen in London which indulged themselves at the corner of a street with a debonair turret. Without taking his luggage from the boot, he went into the Hotel to check in.

After letting Reception know he had arrived, he decided not to see his room immediately, but to walk out and have a proper look at Kilellan on foot. The tales of reconnaissance in the War had always appealed to him, and he thought of himself, as a husband and father of two, as applying on behalf of his family the same principles in peacetime of fieldwork and intelligence.

It was a pretty village, with two relatively understated churches, a great deal of Victorian and Edwardian terracing, and, as he'd noticed from the car, some mansions built with a generalised Arts and Crafts aesthetic. He'd heard that Charles Rennie Mackintosh had designed some of the buildings in Kilellan, demonstrating the wealth of the place. A few of the grand houses used roughcast successfully, with a clean white finish, no doubt using a product of higher quality and with more frequent maintenance than their council estate counterparts.

A solid looking primary school was right at the centre of the village. He had been advised that the school would be inadequate in the next few years if the population of Kilellan was going to grow as expected.

The Association had told him that there were plans to move the school out to what was now farmland. Within a year the fields would start to give way to what would in the end be a large private housing estate. The new school would be a modern flat-roof affair at the end of the estate closest to the old village.

He and his wife Evelyn agreed with the Association that it was an ideal site on which to raise children. Their two boys would not have to walk across a main road to get to school, which would be kitted-out with fresh materials and in all probability would have highly motivated staff. New schools encouraged talent from teachers and children alike. The children would be much closer to the countryside here than they could dream of in the Southeast.

Ford walked out past the railway station, past the gated entrance of Lyle's Woods, clearly once the driveway for an old Renfrewshire manor, and out to the fields. There were two farms. The nearest was still inhabited, and there was a tractor starting up in the yard. He waved across to the driver, but the driver may not have seen him; he did not return the greeting.

Further away, as the land gradually dipped towards a river in the distance, there was a derelict set of buildings. Ford knew they constituted Home Farm, where the first houses were to be built. He and Evelyn had already decided to buy one of the first houses on the estate, simply on the basis of the brochure and the people he had talked to at the Association, but he wanted a physical connection with the place, too.

They had deliberated over the particular design for a fortnight, finally choosing a kind of stepped bungalow that would use the contours of a small hill to nestle into the landscape. Evelyn could see great potential for a rockery, and Ford would make a sandpit for the boys out on the back patio. Still, he wanted to fully command the choice he, in the end, was making on behalf of the family. He wanted to know just what the look and the smell and even the touch of the land was before their home, of hopefully many years, was built there.

He carefully crossed the barbed-wire fence and made his way down to the greenfield site. He knew enough from his childhood not to cross fields directly. Many were still being worked. He walked alongside the fences and hedges until he finally got to the beginning of the overgrown areas of farmland. He knew then that he could just walk wherever he wanted, and he strode into a field of waist-high grass and weeds. Exhilarated by having to force his path through the vegetation, Ford broke into a run, only stopping when his breath began to heave. He held his chest, panting, and looked down at his shoes. They were muddy and had caught leaves and grass seed at the laces.

Once he had caught his breath he looked up. The sleek river, moving in a muscular meander through a pasture that he knew would be untouched by the construction, looked promising for trout. Maybe Alan was old enough now to try fly-fishing? Ford would have to wear gloves and a hat with mufflers for protection! He thought that a crash helmet might be a good investment. As he always said to Evelyn, no one could fault Alan for enthusiasm.

Ford could see now that there was a road leading right up to the old farm: he needn't have gone cross-country. Up on the hills beyond the river there was the village's war memorial, white and barely weathered and, further back, a large pale building that Ford had heard was a kind of borstal.

He breathed in deeply. He picked three pieces of feathery grass for Evelyn and the boys.

He walked back along the farm road and was soon back in the centre of Kilellan.

As he climbed the brae to the Hotel he noticed a small cluster of houses which were clearly council-built. They probably dated from the 1950s. They were in good condition and used a kind of clean dark stone that was in keeping with the rest of Kilellan. There was no roughcast in sight.

When he reached the Hotel he went to take the luggage out of the boot of his car. Before he had the key in the lock he could see that the boot had been jemmied. When he opened the dented lid fully he could see that all his luggage had gone. Even the car jack had been taken.

He now had no fresh clothes, but what he immediately missed was a signet-ring he had bought many years ago, before he had met Evelyn. It had been engraved with a coat of arms the jeweller had taken from a card file and which corresponded to the surname Ford. He had worn it less and less as the fashion changed, but he still took it with him on trips, as if it were a kind of St Christopher.

Ford walked into Reception and asked if he might phone his wife.

Cheggies

All the chestnuts were wobbles of circles, brown eyes of cows not the weight of ball bearings, wooden marbles pouring in a herd of glockenspiel globs out and onto the aircraft aisle. Alive.

'Alan!' said the you-know-whos, and 'O!' said the Lady walking up and down wearing seat material and a hat made from a company flag.

Then the radio said 'We will be landing at Renfrew in the next few minutes. Please sadden your seatbelts and distinguish all minarets.'

'There's one thing I know about cheggies – they're cheggies. Only boys fae Bishopton would call them chessies.

Chessies are for Jessies, right.'

Chestnuts still in their jackets are the green and spiky miniatures of mines with plaques on the promenades of Clyde resorts, like pet heart attacks, like tree-urchins, like the Devil's gobstoppers. Like a big clean mouth of spit (copied in plastic for freebies in Cornflakes packets).

After school when Alan took us cheggying it was late and we saw the pellets of an owl in Lord and Lady's wood. They're just pills of bones like an owl's own Oxo cube of crushed cars, mice, in a scrapyard.

We also saw an owl itself. Flying towards us, pale, face a plate, scanning and not making its call.

'In-all-likelihood a Tawny Snowy Short-Eared Owl,' Alan said.

We climbed some trees and shook some branches but the best method is throwing a stick. Some really very big sticks weren't heavy at all when you went to pick them up. They were like the raw materials for a model glider.

Alan got the most cheggies, but I got the best. It shone, had its own spotlight. Dad said later it was a niner or a tenner, in-all-likelihood.

'Can I plant it in the garden like Alan's from Twyford?'

'It probably wouldn't grow as tall as Alan's.'

'In-all-likelihood?'

Racing Green

What did his mother mean when she said: 'Well then. Lovely! Racing green, please.'

The boy had just come into the kitchen. He had nearly flattened himself bumping into the drop-leaf of the kitchen fitment – what was that doing out? It must be chicken – so he hadn't caught his father's question.

As well as the roast, the air had the benefit of Sunday's gravy and roast potatoes.

His Mum and Dad would answer no questions.

'Aw, go on, tell me. Tell me! Is it just a new dress?'

His mother never had new clothes, not bought ones. She made almost everything herself. She kitted herself out, and she made shirts and play trousers for her sons, as well. Her cast-iron sewing machine occupied one corner of his parents' bedroom. The machine could double for an ornamental table if the Singer was ever swung under and packed away beneath its wooden casing, but it never was. There was too much to have to displace.

The many layers of fabrics in the room were piled so high that, on one side at least, they touched the handle of one of the top windows. To him, the handle was a machine-gun peeping over the top of sandbags. The window faced out across the road to the Armstrongs' split-level bungalow, which was a German bunker of course, when need be.

Maybe Dad was talking about a new length of fabric from Remnant Kings. But why the secrecy?

They had all moved into the dining area at the back of the lounge.

'Are you going to say grace today?'

His mother was changing the subject, but there were the soft yellows and greens and the pale and dark and the rich browns of Sunday dinner and that was something even Alan had to stop for. He was already at the table.

The boy was biddable and agreed.

You didn't have to put your hands together like Assembly, you just had to look down at the edge of the table and half-close your eyes.

G Plan.

The table had slightly rounded edges and, despite the unstained wood of the table top, it had sturdy but graceful lacquer legs. It seemed to match his mother's dressing table, which, like the Singer, was also packed around with brightly-coloured dressmaking material.

'G Plan,' his mother had once said, when he asked her about the similarity. 'They're both G Plan. That goes right back to when your Dad and I were first married.'

He knew this was not a sufficient answer. The information regarding his parents' earlier life was something that sounded like an explanation but was actually the opposite. He had sensed that his mother for once was not in an explaining mood. Perhaps she did not realise that there was more to be said.

G Plan was one of those personal open sesame words that Mum had, like 'Canterbury', where she grew up, or a song she sung at the sink, *Love is a Many Splendoured Thing*. His father's strange first name was another, and Alan's and, he believed, his own. He had not pursued it, but he had an idea that to his mother 'Racing green' was a phrase that held a similar magic.

'For-what-we-are-about-to-receive-may-the-Lord-make-us-truly-thankful,' he said, quickly. 'Amen.'

'Ever thought of a career in broadcasting, son?' his Dad said, shaking his head, eyes heavenwards.

He knew it was a joke, but he couldn't quite work it out. 'Ha ha,' he said, defiantly, as if he did know. He looked sideways at Alan.

'Dad means you maybe said grace a bit quick.'

'Lee. Quick-lee.'

He and Alan now both looked at each other, then copied Dad's heavenwards look. There was not a lot you could do with a dad like Dad.

During the summer holidays, Alan and his friends would go and pick raspberries in the woods for Mum to make jam. The woods were right at the end of the estate, where new houses were being built. Alan could jump up and hang from the top of a doorframe in the unfinished homes, or get right up into a roof space. He also collected silver metal discs that he punched out from the electric junction boxes. He used them as loose change for the one-armed bandits whenever the Fair came to the village.

'Don't use fake coins on a machine too many times – you don't want to win them back again!'

Alan was very good at advising him on matters like that. Personally speaking, though, he preferred to know about a thing rather than actually do it. He couldn't imagine dreeping from loft-spaces himself, but he always tried to go along with Alan's gang just to see what they got up to. His school friends lived on the other side of the village and during the holidays he wasn't allowed to go along the main road to go and see them (Philip next door went to a private school and they didn't get on). His mother was even beginning to think twice about letting him play up at the Mill Pool.

Normally Alan had to be begged to take him along anywhere, but his mother must have had a word with him about picking raspberries, because Alan wasn't just letting him walk alongside, he even made sure he had enough containers and a bottle of squash.

He thought it was interesting that Alan's friends had all different types of plastic containers to put the raspberries in, including Andrea who had a plastic bag. He and Alan had old ice-cream containers, but it looked as if some of the bowls the others had were actually custom-made for raspberry collecting. They didn't have any faded label, or the scuffed mark where an attempt had been made to remove one. Some of the plastic bowls were round, and they had a special lid with a tab to help you take it off more easily.

Alan didn't think this was interesting.

They had been picking for hours and he had got slightly separated from the main group. They were working on a steep slope in the woods, and the stands of wild raspberries were high above his head. The gang had instinctively moved down the slope in a slow, systematic sweep, but he could not see properly where they had gone, and although he could just hear them, he wasn't sure where they were.

He had begun to get worried. In trying to catch up with them he had stumbled a little, having taken a direction he had, frankly, guessed. As he grabbed around, trying to stop himself from falling completely, he caught a few raspberry thorns under his nails. He didn't want to shout out, because he wanted to be as much a part of the gang as possible, and anyway it didn't hurt that much. It wasn't as if they were the hard thorns that brambles had, and he wasn't a crybaby.

After that, because he had not felt safe going downwards, he had shuffled along the slope instead. He had soon reached a swathe of tall bracken, again over his head, but easier going underfoot, and he had finally come through to another stand of raspberries.

He knew straight away that something was odd about them. It wasn't just that they were untouched. It was... to do with colour. An absence of any deep red, any red at all. And something else, something it took a few moments to realise, and was all the more peculiar for it.

The berries were yellow.

At first, he thought they weren't ripe. Then he looked at them closely. He could see that there were unripe ones alongside the yellows: these were green just like ordinary ones.

Was this what his mother meant by 'racing green'?

In any case, the ripe raspberries were soft to touch, just like red ones were, and they had a sweet smell not unlike the ones he knew. They must at least belong to the same family.

He stopped short of tasting them.

He was thinking of the book Dad had bought – 'This is for all of us' – from the *Reader's Digest*. Poisonous berries and toadstools glared out of its pages like evil spirits. In particular, there was a full colour picture of the speckled red and white toadstool known as Fly Agaric. With its garish look and the name's echo of arsenic (everyone knew Robin Hood had been murdered by drinking arsenic), that page had given him nightmares. Most deadly things seemed to be brightly coloured, as well. Think of tigers and wasps. Gobstoppers could suffocate you, too. The whole book had given him a severe and general suspicion of the ostentatiously odd.

Alan enjoyed reading the book. He said it was almost as

good as Dad's *Home Doctor*, which Alan said he mustn't read until he was older.

The yellow raspberries were something that surely Alan would know about. Knowing the way he looked at the world, he might even think they were a great find, even if they could kill you.

He felt it wouldn't look stupid if he called out now.

'Alan!' he shouted, 'I've found some poison!'

It had been a good day's berry-picking. Their containers were full, and they'd have to think about a quite different part of the woods tomorrow because today's bushes were bare.

Dad would be back from work by now, and they'd get some extra pocket money for bringing in so many pounds of fruit. The yellow berries were a definite plus, as well, although Alan wasn't completely sure if you could make jam out of them. They weren't dangerous, apparently. They were a good find. There weren't very many of them, so maybe they'd just have them with some cream. To be honest, they'd both been stuffing themselves with raspberries of both kinds all afternoon, so they hoped Mum went for the jam option.

As the gang walked through the estate, in a tired line right across the road, their friends would one by one say bye and head off to their homes. Finally, all that remained were the two boys and Andrea, who lived nearby. Andrea was carrying her bag of raspberries across her back like a sack of coal.

'Has your Dad got a new car?' she asked them.

They both looked up. Parked on their drive was a brand-new, bright purple, Capri.

The boys were astonished. It might as well have been a crocodile. In fact, it looked liked a crocodile: a huge purple crocodile.

They quickly said bye to Andrea – 'See you tomorrow!' – 'See ya!' – and rushed up to the house. Andrea did not seem hurt by this.

Dad and Mum were at the lounge's long window, looking out at the car. They came out of the house when they saw the boys running up. The boys had put their containers down on the drive's red stones, and were both peering in at the dashboard.

'Is it ours, Dad?'

'What's the top speed?'

They both liked it. Dangerous things were fine, if they belonged to you.

'It certainly is ours. It's one of the first Capris in Scotland, so they tell me. The top speed of all cars in this country is seventy miles an hour, and that can only be realised on a motorway.' Dad always said this about a car's speed. It was his attempt to educate them about careful driving and speed limits. Even a Lamborghini's top speed in this country is seventy miles an hour and that can only be realised on a motorway.

'And such a lovely shade of *green*,' Mum said.

The boy didn't understand.

'They just couldn't do it in time, love. So I thought you'd like it in another feminine colour.'

There was a pause, and Mum noticed the raspberries.

'Oh thanks, boys. They're lovely. And yellow ones, too! Especially sweet.'

'John found the yellow ones,' Alan said.

'At least you two know what colours your mother likes,' she said, with a look at Dad.

There was a pause.

'Dad,' John said, 'ever thought of a career in broadcasting?'

The Mansion

He had cleaned his teeth, sucked the tap, slooshed and spat. In fresh pyjamas, blue, unruled, he skipped down the old stairs of their new house, missing every second – stretch – third step.

He has to stretch himself.

He ran into the lounge.

'Night, Mum. Night, Dad.'

A kiss for Mum. She paid it back.

Dad just said goodnight and then his family nickname. In bed, you could see tonight the curtains were no good. Summer light got through, and beyond the now-and-then of a breeze in the vast sycamores, a pack of boys, girls you guessed in goals, moved a football with their shouts.

He got up and walked to the window. He unfolded the old shutters out of the wall, and pressed them into darkness. He swivelled the small hook.

He walked slowly to his bed, feeling his way, and lay down. No, there were still slits of light, but he turned away from the window and was asleep in a few minutes.

As he woke he remembered he didn't have to wear his uniform today.

Until yesterday he'd been a Bluebottle, from Kilellan Primary. The private boys, in red, were The Squashed Tomatoes. The Cucumbers were the girls at St Columba's. They had green blazers and green gym kits, and long hair in bulldog clips. Even so, they weren't Catholics.

He didn't like salads.

After the summer holidays he'd to start at the school closest to their new house, Kilpeter Primary.

From now on he didn't have six legs.

By leaping down the right and left edges of the stairs, he made sure he didn't touch the thick brown underfelt, their only covering so far. He could hear Mum and Dad talking in the kitchen, which was odd.

'She's right, he is "arrogant".'

Dad was still in the house. Now that they had moved, it must mean he didn't have to rush his breakfast.

'But he's also shy. Anyway, can you really call a little kid "arrogant"? That seems on the pompous side to me. Typical Miss Bytheway! Hul-lo?'

Dad sounded as if this was funny ha-ha *and* funny peculiar. He was in the old clothes he always wore about the house.

'You'll be late for work, Dad!' the boy laughed. This was what the news on Mum's radio would call 'unheard of'.

One of the heavy red oven's covers was up. Three pots seemed to gossip together there, cooking away on the metal plate. He would make the Aga into a submarine's torpedo launcher at some point.

'Have you had your breakfast?' he added.

Dad and Mum looked at each other.

'Son, it's still the evening. Have a drink of water and get back to bed.'

Grayling

You wondered about grayling. Your father caught very few – he was always fishing for another kind of fish – and when he did land one he'd say to you, 'That's a nice grayling, son, would you like to put him back?' Fishes were boys, ships were women.

They were always put back, even a sizeable catch.

Grayling were the sound you'd better not take out of the place, the hard g and its gravely r. The Gryffe guarded its grayling. Dad had to lift you across a cattle grid to get to the right river pools, so you had a glimpse of the earning in that sound. It was lucky that as you got taller your feet would also grow lengthwise. That's what seemed to have happened to Mum and Dad, so you'd master the iron trap yourself, eventually.

Did cows hurt their hoofs trying to go on holiday?

'Wait a second son while I set the bag down – I'm coming back for you!'

Grayling made the same kind of sense as your surname: Ford was a lightweight car and a shallow part of the river. You and the fish were a word, and you were both a thing.

Grayling was also the name of something else. It was almost the colour grey. Brown trout were not really brown – they were a darkly-speckled bronze, with pink and soft reds – and it was the same for grayling. They had silvery, greenish tinges, with faint purple tones at the top, and plain white at the belly. If the colour grey was alive it would be the colour of grayling: they should make a cartoon about fish and colour. They could make grayling be grey's children, like ducks have ducklings.

The lanky tall fin wouldn't last once the fish grew up: maybe they'd become salmon.

You could explain the name by most folk not seeing them close up. They wouldn't be good fishermen like your Dad, so they probably only saw the fish for a second, from a bridge where they'd parked their car. Most things looked dull when you saw them like that.

You yourself had never noticed a thirty-mile-an-hour sign lying in the riverbed. It must have been there for years. Dad never mentioned it until one day, when you already had two trout in the bag, he said, 'Yes, great fishing here. All the fish have to go slow.' He just pointed downstream, and you saw for the first time the pole and its big circle and the plain-as-day number.

You could not bring grayling back into the house. Your mother also said you should never give a knife, so your father had to pay you a penny if Mum got you to give him a chisel for his birthday. Grayling were jinxed, which meant they were lucky from their point of view. Dad pushed a knife into a trout's brain.

'Shame really – they say grayling taste like thyme. You know, thyme the herb? But we'd better not take him.'

So you got to hold the fish and place it in the river – head facing upstream to get its breath back – and it slipped back into its world and out of yours.

Kidnapping Kenneth

Eddie Chatterjee, John Craig and I were the British Spy Agency.

Our main achievements were the three booklets we'd made for ourselves, one each. They were a hybrid of a passport and the kind of security badge that authenticates officers of the law and men from the utilities. Eddie put them together from scrap paper that Craigie's dad had brought home from work. Eddie was good at art, and he drew cartoon 'photographs' of us. I gave each of us a fake name, and an exotic personal history. But the soft pencil we used made the drawings and text smudge within a month.

We also conducted a successful commando raid on the Major's vast estate, when we mapped the pet cemetery, sawmill, and his private air raid shelter.

Kenneth wasn't like Eddie or Craigie. They lived on an orangey new private estate, which I'd played in when it had been just birches and straggly grass. He lived on the Sharps, a much greyer affair, a council scheme placed firmly away from the centre of the village and well away from where Eddie and Craigie lived. It was a vast, awkward, angular crescent. From the air, it must have looked like a huge coat-hanger without the hook.

At one end of the scheme was a large house for those the polite called the handicapped. At the other end there was a more recent structure, the old folks' home.

High above them all was a grassy hill, common land in the main, except for the west side where there were large private houses in substantial grounds. The kids from the Sharps called them 'the Mansions'.

That's where I lived. My father had been promoted when I was eight and we had moved away from the village of Kilellan to this one a few miles away, Kilpeter. I was a lord of my own wee manor there, living in the impressive church cast-off 'The Old Manse'.

Eddie's father was an anaesthetist. Craigie's, like mine, was a manager: his dad worked at a computer plant down near Greenock; my father was in the construction industry, building the latest versions of the Sharps across central Scotland.

Kenneth's dad drove lorries for one of the distribution companies operating out of the Airport. In fact, everyone in our class had been given a sticker from the firm, brought in by Kenneth one Christmas. It featured the company's brave red and black truck-in-an-arrow shape. My sticker must still be on the burgundy tiles of the fireplace my father boarded up to make the bedroom less draughty.

Kenneth's parents were from Skye, but he'd always lived in the village. He went back to the island for most of the summer. When my family had come to Kilpeter he was chosen to befriend me, but we had never become great pals. Craigie and I thought it would be a good idea to kidnap him.

First of all, we needed a place to kidnap him *to*. In my garden we had made a den from some of the logs lying along the drive, so that was the natural choice. A Scots pine had been felled by a team of gasmen who'd accidentally sliced its roots when they were putting in pipes to the house. Dad had explained to them that the heating ran on oil, but somehow he'd been persuaded it would be good to keep his options open.

Neither Eddie nor Craigie knew Kenneth well, and it would have appeared odd if they had called on him. Obviously, it wasn't safe in any case for Eddie Chatterjee to go into the Sharps.

I still spoke to Kenneth, though usually competitively, since we were both near the top of the class (as was his twin sister, Mary). For that reason, I was to go down the hill, knock on his door, and lure him out.

By the time I'd made the five-minute walk, across the grassland that is now a levelled and unloved blaze football pitch, I was praying Kenneth would be out.

Mary answered the door. She seemed a little puzzled, but perhaps also pleased.

'Yes, I'll just go and get him. Ken-neth!'

Kenneth came down and said hello, put his brown vinyl jacket on and came out. We started walking back up the hill.

'We went to Skye, this year.' I said. 'It was great! We were attacked by Arctic terns!'

Kenneth looked at me. 'Did you see any of the seals?'

'This is our den,' Eddie said.

For a few seconds, Kenneth seemed delighted to know our secret. As we had walked up to the back gate, he had been pleased to be invited into the British Spy Agency. It was also the first time in over a year since he'd been up at the Old Manse, and I think he felt that I had had quite a change of heart; that I regretted us not getting on better together.

I was just wondering if maybe we should just call the kidnap off but, to everyone's surprise, Craigie shouted out, 'And this is our ammo!' He whipped out a water pistol and started shooting him.

This was not in the plan. We had agreed to imprison and interrogate the prisoner first. But clearly it was too late now, so Eddie and I reached behind a tree and picked up our squeezy-bottle machine-guns. We surrounded Kenneth and joined in the execution.

Kenneth put his hands up over his glasses, bowed his head and shoulders a little and just stood there. His jacket repelled most of the water, but his hair and sweatshirt collar and the groin of his jeans were quickly drenched. After a few seconds, though, he crouched further down , his body all tensing, then through the gap between Craigie and me. We went to grab him, but couldn't get a proper hold because of the guns we were carrying.

He ran, fast.

Only Eddie could have caught him, but we all just jeered instead.

'Teuchter!' Craigie shouted, and Eddie and me joined in.

Because our parents never got to hear it about it, I don't think Kenneth could have told his mother and father. There seemed to be no change in his relationship to me at school, either, not even a look of reproach.

Much later, Eddie, Craigie and I buried the British Spy Agency with its fuzzy identity cards in a biscuit tin coffin, a stone's throw from the pet cemetery and air raid shelter in the heart of the Major's grounds.

Crash

His lips and teeth had got confused. A couple of teeth were showing through to the outside. Inside, others were at wrong angles. Weak. They might be falling out any minute, and his tongue had to keep testing them to see if that was going to happen.

His top lip was bloated, and tight and cut. His lower lip was dry and tender and clogged with the paste of blood. He felt like he was wearing new lips over the old ones.

Inside his mouth, it was the same: yet another pair of lips, internal this time, making his mouth smaller than it used to be. They were pushing his jaw out of shape and even his breathing had to be thought about now. It was not the same, breathing.

The policeman was saying OK.

OK.

OK, son.

OK, son, blow into the bag please.

John, my younger son, was watching a film on television so it was he who took Alan's call. It was gone midnight, so heaven knows what the boy wonder had been doing this time. That late, it wasn't as if he could have been driving straight home after last orders, though obviously he would be tanked up. And he wasn't even coming back from the village, because he was calling from Ferrier's Homes – that's a sort of nineteenth century new town built for orphans, and still used as such at the time. A couple of miles out of his way at any rate.

I got out of my pyjama bottoms and put my underpants and fishing waterproofs on, and a jumper over my pyjama jacket. John wanted to come as well, which I thought twice about – I didn't know how bad Alan would be – but I said OK.

The car started at first go, though John had to fiddle around to find the seatbelt clip. I switched on the inside light so he could get sorted out. Bookish, that one.

We didn't talk in the ten minutes it took to get to Ferrier's, except to hope for the best and think out loud, 'What's he done this time?' – but I was glad of the company. John is the same when you go fishing. Hopeless, really –

can't tie a fly, and his casting action is all jerks – but good to have along, when he settles and does nothing.

Alan had told him he was on the main road, so I just kept driving. In fact, we had almost got through Ferrier's when we saw the car. It had smashed into a low wall on a bend. You could see straight away that the car had been travelling too fast and he had just tried to iron out a corner that could not be ironed out.

It was like one of those recent cruise-control accidents. Not that the old banger had cruise control. The whole of the bonnet was crumpled. Metal was folded over the nearside wheel, which was out of shape. The way the metal cut into the tyre was appalling: you realised how finely balanced a car's materials were, how dangerous it all was, driving within an equilibrium of softnesses and the hard and the sharp.

All around the front of the car and on the road and roadside there was the coarse powder of the windscreen. John says it was like a sprinkling of coconut ice.

I drove past, round the corner, and parked next to the patrol car that had come into view. The passenger door was open and Alan was sitting sideways on the seat, half in the car, half out. Two policemen were standing over him. One of them had his notebook out, another had something shiny in his hand that had caught my headlights. For a second, the police looked like waiters, taking Alan's order.

When I walked up to them, I recognised the officer taking notes. He had been involved in an accident investigation on one of my sites not that long ago.

'Hello, Mr Ford. This one's yours then?'

I made a point of speaking to Alan before I answered his question.

'Are you alright, son?'

Alan could not speak very well. He had his hand against his mouth, and his face was a mess of blood.

'These bastards are trying to force that into my mouth!' he said, shrilly. He sounded as if he had no teeth.

What had glinted in my headlights was a Breathalyser. The other policeman was guiltily holding it by his side, almost behind his back.

'It's the law,' he said.

Before I could reply, the ambulance arrived. The paramedics and I were able to get Alan quickly away, though he was swearing at everyone. John and I followed the ambulance for the twenty minute drive to the infirmary, where they cleaned the boy up and put dissolving stitches into his top lip.

When the police called round the next day, Alan was contrite and I was apologetic.

They pressed no charges.

Recurrer

'Hold my hand.'

The boy's mother took it anyway, hurrying across the shallows at the entrance to the petrol station.

In the new bay, the wire rigging of yachts moored to footballs jigged frantically but in silence. Vision was blurred in the rain, but it was understood that the old railway station must now be completely submerged.

They reached the bridge.

In the white fencing and the merely scratchy prickles growing through it, in the road mended with rubber dinghy glue, in – now they were across – the secure shop terrace and the homes above it (Alastair lives on top of a greengrocer), they realised that the new harbour town was still Kilellan.

A new Kilellan.

Until this morning the village had been several miles from the sea.

'Hold my hand.'

He *was* holding her hand, now, but he pressed it again, meaning *I am*, and they crossed Lochwinnoch Road just past the police station and its glowing blue-lamp sweets.

There was no checkpoint at the Lodge. They went straight on into Lyle's Woods. The road was just crammed rubble and pools of brown colloid.

A sense of police sirens – they both jolted, but could hear no sound.

His mother gently tugged at him, steering him a little. She said nothing, but they moved off on to a side path.

The track was rich in dark nettles at its edges and, further in, there was a wall of vagrant raspberry canes whose silver undersides twitched like foil. You couldn't see what was round the next turn.

They were too tired.

They staggered off the path into a mass of woody stems and foliage.

They crouched down. Three tiny birds trembled on slender green branches above them.

The ground here was only damp, but cold heavy drops

of water, collected by the leaves above their heads, fell close by, and sometimes on to their hair and on to their faces. They could feel the weight of their own bodies balanced on the muscles of their legs, on the exhausted hinges of their knees.

Men in full-length oiled coats stopped on the path some distance in front of them, unsure of themselves. They seemed to decide neither to go on, nor to go back.

Then the men stepped into the undergrowth. As if dancing to police guidelines, they edged methodically closer, beating back the vegetation, heading perhaps a fraction to one side of the boy and his mother.

3

The Kilellan
Hydropathic Establishment

Thank you very much, Mr Caird. I shall try to live up to such a glowing introduction. And may I say how very honoured I feel to have been invited to speak to the Members of this esteemed Society, especially as I believe I will be the first lady ever to give such an address. It is also a very gratifying attendance tonight.

I have heard so much about your work, which is so in consonance with the activities of the Hydropathic, and I regret very much that I have not yet had the opportunity to become a Member. That is an error I shall certainly correct, with your blessing, by the end of this evening.

The Kilellan Hydropathic Hotel was opened on the first of May 1880 as the Kilellan Hydropathic Establishment. Designed by the architects Watsons of Regent Street, Glasgow, it was intended to be a holiday retreat for businessmen and their wives. Many of these would already have been aware, by virtue of other well-publicised improvements, that Kilellan was not only a place of considerable countryside charm but was now simply blossoming in comforts, and comforts, in the case of the Hydropathic, appointed to a very high standard indeed.

As you know, the Railway had reached Kilellan some years beforehand, and what was in many ways little more than a rural hamlet had then started to grow its fine crop of mansions, the property of enterprising ship-owners and cotton mill directors. A splendid golf course was cut from the hillside within a decade or so of the Hydropathic's official opening and, notwithstanding Kilellan's great natural beauty and charm, together our two great institutions remain the village's two outstanding attractions.

For a time, I'm told, there was some question as to whether Queen Victoria Herself would enjoy Kilellan as her official Scottish residence rather than the no doubt romantic but surely inferior Balmoral, and the rumour, I'm sure, did no harm to the village despite the regrettable outcome.

In those days there was no particularly Celtic sentiment abroad in the country. Records show that the Board considered there to be no gain in emphasising Kilellan's Hibernian roots, being founded, it is thought, by a saint, St Eileen of Antrim and Iona. On the contrary, such a tactic might in all probability attract such guests who were more artistic in temperament than conscientious as to the satisfaction of outstanding fees.

However, if Kilellan had now forged its own Spa, for the taking of waters and that general therapy which pertains to the easing of mild afflictions of body and mind by other hydropathic means, then, without adopting the example of Lourdes in degree or catholicity of complaint, here would be something that would certainly be a credit to the village, and of considerable advertising potency in Kilellan's official handbook. Indeed, the name 'Hydropathic' had been chosen especially to underline the recent medical research that we now know conclusively proves that such a Spa, with 128 bedrooms, Turkish sauna and shampooing room, can offer nothing but health-giving qualities.

It could only be taken as a compliment that the Establishment's ever-widening reputation for good health sometimes made it a target for local witticisms. In the popular mind of 1900 there seemed to be a conflict between the bar and restaurant side of the service, on the one hand, and the invigorating physical facilities on offer on the other. More recently it has even been said, in jocular fashion no doubt, that the principal exercise guests take is that which is derived from the walk they are compelled to undertake when they surmount the infamous incline that lies between the Railway Station and the Hydropathic itself. This, as I'm sure you know, is a humourism based on a wilful misconception, propagated originally I may conjecture by resentful ex-serving staff and the proprietors of the then failing and now defunct Ranfurly Hotel, on the edge of our good neighbour-village, Bridge of Weir.

I don't have to remind this audience that most of our guests who arrive by the conveyance of the Railway have the good commercial sense on disembarkation to avail themselves of the complimentary pony and trap.

By way of digression, may I also say how pleasing it is to see that the civic guardians of Bridge of Weir have recently decided to concentrate more on what their fair village does best. I wish Mr Maclay every success with his Leather Capital of Scotland campaign.

However, to return to our theme, Kilellan's rise has certainly been spectacular, but it has not always been straightforward. The Hydropathic has followed the same pattern. In the early years, even the Hydropathic suffered one or two lurches of adjustment, the reconfigurations between idealism and the strictures of necessity so characteristic of pioneering institutions. Chief of these was its bankruptcy in 1883, put right by a new managerial expertise of considerable modernity, to which, several decades later, we are still indebted. The transition from our service as a military hospital in the recent War, when our Country demanded much of us, has been smoother than we could have hoped, and it is a point of quiet pride that, notwithstanding the unfortunate case of poor Corporal Woodsley, several of our wartime patients have already returned as voluntary guests.

Under the present proprietors, a number of telephones have been added at various strategic locations throughout the building; a rolling programme of bedroom refurbishment continues, and our resident Director of Health, Dr Schwartz, devises evermore inventive health routines, literally keeping everyone on their toes. For well-earned relaxation come evening time, our range of cocktails would make New York and Paris blush, and our menu rivals the fare of the best restaurants of the Empire. It is no overstatement to say that the high Gothic tower of the Kilellan Hydropathic is regarded as a beacon of good health and earned enjoyment across the wealth-creating world.

Finally, before I return to my seat and allow Mr Caird to field questions that I will do my very best to answer, I hope I may be allowed to say something regarding the coming vote on Thursday at Lang's Halls.

Although one has a good deal of sympathy with the ideals of the Temperance Movement, a good deal of sympathy, especially in the light of the recent reports of degrading behaviour witnessed in the public houses of our aforementioned dear neighbour-village, I have confidence that Kilellan's voters on Thursday will trust in the sensible natures of the overwhelming majority of their own kind, and, of course in the civilised predispositions of the Hydropathic's clientele, visitors who contribute so much to the local economy. I am sure that most will agree with the proprietors of the Hydropathic, among whose number I am privileged to count myself, that the current proposal for a general prohibition on the selling of alcohol throughout the village and country district must be defeated on the grounds of plain and simple common sense. 'Everything in moderation,' as the good doctor says! I'm sure that there will be a *sane* result on Thursday, and that the Hydropathic's glory days lie ahead of it, not in the past.

Thank you again, for inviting me to speak tonight.

Unsigned transcript of a speech by Miss Abigail Campbell, manageress of the Kilellan Hydropathic Establishment, 1910-1920, given to the Kilellan Society in May 1920.

This speech, recovered by a schoolboy among the ruins of the old Kilellan Hydropathic Establishment in 1975, gives an outline of the Hydro's history and hints at its catastrophic decline. Despite Miss Campbell's appeal to the 'sensible natures' of the people of Kilellan, the electorate were persuaded by the strong temperance lobby of the day. They voted overwhelmingly to declare the village and country district a no-alcohol area.

Later that year Miss Campbell left for Zurich with Günter Schwartz, where they established a successful sanatorium for industrialists with psychological problems. There is no evidence to suggest that Miss Campbell was ever in fact a proprietor of the Hydro, or that Schwartz was a medical doctor.

The new management of the Hydro accepted a severely limited drinks licence, and the Establishment endured a number of decades of slow decline. It served the same function in the Second World War as it had in the First: it was a military hospital. The 'Corporal Woodsley tragedy' to which Miss Campbell alludes was the Corporal's suicide, the source of a number of sensational stories in the *Kilellan Observer*. Woodsley's suicide note, which does not survive, was reportedly in the form of a passionate poem dedicated to the manageress.

By the end of the 1960s the Hydro was derelict, and in 1974 almost all of the building was demolished. At first, dynamite failed to destroy the tower, but the respite lasted only a few years. In 1977 a firm of oil engineers finally toppled it. The whole site was then redeveloped as a small private housing estate. Kilellan's alcohol bylaws were revoked in 1989, when the disused railway station was converted and re-opened as The Old Railway Arms.

Answers to an Interview

Let me answer your question another way. If you think I'm speaking mainly as the artist you believe I am, this interview means next to nothing to me. It will only add something to the understanding of the paintings if your readers appreciate art essentially as the language of exhibition catalogues and painting titles, as histories of art and biographies, as the language of interviews with the artist. If paintings are only arrangements of colour on which to focus your attention while you contemplate the world of words, then, alright, this interview is going to help. Because of Martha, and it's because of Martha I can't let this just be a publicity thing, though it has to be that, too.

People have to see her paintings.

Because my work being part of it, out here – there has been no railway line since the eighties – might not be enough. That's why the publicity. I certainly see the irony of my work being a lure to get folk to see Martha's, but that is the commercial reality.

Martha said quite a while ago that one of my problems was that my work was too text-based, that it was not driven visually. She first mentioned it around the time of the Renfrewshire Installations. So I've tried to take that further as a critique not just of my own work, which I've come to accept – I think I accept it – but of how the whole art business functions. But here I am today in the unwanted situation of delivering yet another text, and, worse than that, it's actually occasioned by Martha's work. By her death.

It's her work this is all about, even if it is a joint show. And her work was always so unliterary, so unprefaced, so in itself without text.

Surprisingly enough, she had a soft spot for manifestos, even though she was not keen on 'literary art', or badly made conceptual work, to take the most obvious kind.

Her collection – they're part of the School's library now, and I use them now and again for teaching – dates mostly from the first years of the last century – the Italian and Russian Futurists – but does go right up to our own Kilbarchan Misinformers. She said they assert across art –

they can't, obviously, wholly or wholeheartedly underwrite the art itself. I think what she meant was that even manifestos in earnest play the game of a rhetoric of assertion, so even those that speak directly in so-called plain speech are defeated in one sense by their own urge to force linguistic meaning. So the most transparently-worded manifestos become the most tangential.

Manifestos are also against what goes by the name of theory, even if they mobilise theoretical language. They actually share a good deal with biography – that sense of activating existing structures of language – 'after that, she...' – although it's usually those who prefer a biographical approach to the interpretation of art who regard themselves as not political, not theoretical – it's usually those kinds of people who are against the manifesto.

Of course, good theories must make reliable predictions. That's the test of a theory. To my knowledge, 'Art theory' hasn't happened yet.

One of Martha's favourite phrases was 'Art is lost for words.' I like the Charles Schultz echo, and she thought, in the end, I was a cartoonist trying to be an artist, that there was too much of a soft centre, a just-so-ness at the heart of my work.

But she loved cartoons, so maybe it was a kind of compliment.

She had me sew that phrase for her, sampler style, with Adam and Eve either side of the Tree of Knowledge, with the words above, in gold entwined with green.

We used to give each other birthday presents that we'd

make to each other's design. She always made me fashion parodies of my own work. Though this was the last present I gave her, it was based on the Erskine Bridge triptych from thirty years ago.

Yes, she knew even my post-grad stuff, a lot of early work made before we met. I don't know where that painting is hanging now. You couldn't say it was well known! She said it had meant a lot to her, that it was a bridge for her – not across a river, but, with the dissolving edges in the picture, and the dappled handling of the Clyde and of the air, a bridge between the water and the sky above it. The biblical echo was a mistake, the bible's history now, even in Scotland, but I can see how its particular angle, from the water level up to the striding columns of the bridge, would have appealed to her.

I didn't know what I was doing then.

When the public commissions are finished, when we're over all this. You don't get over this. Not knowing what you're doing has a lot going for it.

She'd make me use a medium I wasn't used to, so that time it was needle and thread. She'd never sewed herself.

I guess she taught me a lot. I wouldn't have agreed to direct the Abbey's Threads project without having had to take embroidery seriously beforehand. She made me confront the ignorance of my hands. In accepting the commission it was important I had already started to learn about sewing – more important than being in any way spiritual.

I enjoy embroidery, and have made more sampler-style works since. Para-religious.

I'm not sure. For me, what I actually sew – it's for myself – it's a private art. They're hanging in the house. I still paint! But yes, in a few years, maybe I'll see if they amount to anything.

A self-portrait, a portrait of Martha.

It was always the same. I asked her for the same thing. That's over twenty portraits. But she said I had to sketch the design first, like she had to for me. That was the only time she'd sit for me, though she didn't always consent even then.

For quite a few years she'd just give me a photo of herself to make my sketch from, for her to go and make my rough design – the sketch I was going to give her as a rough for the present she was going to give to me. You get all these layers.

Her photo would be taken on a cheap camera, in a photo booth, or suchlike. One was one of those plastic holiday cameras that are waterproof, for the seaside or the swimming pool. Of course, the snap with that one was of her in the bath. She was wearing a shower cap – which she never does. Did.

There's now an instant camera called the Joycam – the photos are too small and you don't get many in a cartridge.

She'd have loved the Joycam.

My portrait, in charcoal – not her medium, either. I wanted her to make a small painting from the sketch – of herself – but she didn't want to. Instead she took the actual sketch and worked up a denser portrait over it – but a portrait of me. She'd obliterate my sketch – you could see that there was a face beneath the face, but I think only I could have known the ghost was her.

I don't have them any more.

They haven't been found.

It did hurt, at the time. It took me a few years to see she was right and we weren't getting on well. It was during this time she began her bathroom paintings.

It's not an inconsistency, me babbling here this afternoon. Because, I know it's Martha, Martha, but these paintings – they're –

I think the public commissions have to stop. Martha never did a commission in her life.

It's not that the public they're intended for are a problem – it's the administrators who say they're acting on their behalf. And I'm not being holier than thou, here. I don't need the money – I haven't needed it since the *Saints' Towns* series. The problem is that the commissions appeal to me. They appeal to me. They're attractive to those parts of me that I should really keep out of my art.

The Paisley Patterns are almost literally comic strips – I'm not, I think, offending anyone when I say that – so you could say I'm going with my natural artistic inclination there, and – I should say – I've had nothing but help from the Abbey and the Council people. They've been remarkably generous, not just with the money but with their time. Which is amazing, considering the flak they're still getting over the Installations.

It's been my favourite commission, but I think it'll be my last. There are some sketches for it in the show – they made Martha smile, even when she was very ill.

Great artists can work, or have to work, for authority – Michelangelo etcetera – but I guess I'm closer – to Rothko on that, and Martha Nicholson.

I'm not taking anything away from her when I say I knew myself, five, no, ten years ago, that there was something wrong with the work, wrong in the way she described. Despite everything I could do to direct those coming into the gallery away from the textual filters, the work itself was encouraging textual reading. Reading.

It's five years since my paintings had titles, three years since I abandoned the numbered series, because people were getting numerological about them. '"3" eh?, very Celtic, the Trinity, oh yes, of course.' '"13", oh, brooding, very brooding.'

And reproductions of the paintings are as bad. That's why for a while now I've invited art students here at the Tanneries to fill my exhibition catalogues with their work, rather than have snaps of my paintings – at least the catalogues are stimulating interest in unseen work that way. We've had quite a bit of take-up from galleries since I started doing that, especially in Chicago and New York. Tanneries art sells across the world.

For the joint show, simply because of the scarcity of Martha's work, we did things differently. The catalogue reproduces almost all of Martha's paintings, the surviving excerpts of her diary, and a word or two about the Macmillan charity.

None of my paintings are in the catalogue.

I thought my work in those years, even ignoring the titles, was all too text-based. It was either collaborative – most obviously with the sculptures made with the *Hydro Hotel* poets (no offence to them) – or the work was encouraging too much of a narrative reading, the history of Anytown, the life of him or her.

Maybe it isn't a language problem, just a problem of simplification. The Hillman Avenger sculpture is a good example. To me, now, it's language caught in Renfrewshire's net – the dead car factory, the siting of the work on the hill where the Celtic cross once was, the use of the Renfrew scrapyard. Not only was it a dubious pun placed in the centre of all that – language again – it was using the cliché of 'mapping' that characterises so much under-realised twentieth century art and theory. Borders of this, and geographies of that. Topography – honestly. Maybe only the gerund and the idea of 'Invention' are used more. It gets you down, such a level of disimagination.

I'm glad the Avenger was vandalised, that there's still no money to put it back on its plinth. It looks great, toppled, halfway down the hill, even if the *Record* does say it's a danger to 'the little children'.

A girl, twenty, and a boy, just coming up to his fourteenth birthday.

I'd rather not tell you their names.

I like cafés with benches and couches! The metaphoric couch eh? But I wouldn't say they influenced me.

Very top-tennish that question. Martha used to say autistic children – and adults – are characterised by an obsessive interest in simple language systems, especially lists. She said it's very Sunday papers.

Proust, *Young Hearts Run Free, Midnight Train to Georgia*, I don't know. Not just art.

Artists can listen to music and read poetry, surely. As long as they don't sing or go all bardic. Well, not really. It's a beautiful thing to sing, to write, even badly. To listen and to read.

Vermeer, certainly. I'm not a monumentalist, actually. Bonnard, of course. We both loved Vermeer and Bonnard. In our household they both went without saying.

She always denied it was the name. Marthe isn't Martha, after all. But she also didn't want to appear under the same language spell she thought I was under, so maybe there is something in the coincidence.

I see the last five years of her paintings as, yes, emerging from a fascination with Bonnard's paintings of Marthe, Marthe in the bath. 'Claustrophobia or Celebration?' might be a headline I guess. Or 'Pattern, pattern, pattern.'

To begin with, she was probably spending as much time in the bathroom as her near-namesake was. We were all very worried – we didn't know if it was mental or physical. It wasn't as if she was taking her easel in with her. Hours lying in the bath.

The kids were maddened by it. There had always been battles between them over the bathroom when they were getting ready for school, but this was every day, and not with each other but with their own mother! We had to have the immersion heater on all the time, and Martha was buying skincare creams and essential oils practically in bulk.

But then she shut herself away in her studio, right at the top of the Tanneries, and slowly the paintings emerged. Although they are still pretty disturbing, even with all that radiance, to be honest they came as a great relief to us. They back-classified those mad times as information gathering, as research.

Bonnard's off-centrings, his comparatively hard dividing lines – they've gone through the graphic design of Gauguin's cloisonné to something more fingertippy, more sensuous –

compartments in works that are otherwise suffused by shimmer, the cool of a bathroom in a warm climate. Martha reverses the weather conditions, of course! His near annihilation of the face (could he even draw female faces?), his sense of the eye taking in not just what it focuses on but all the fuzzed colour around the point of perception, the intricate patterning of what is not wholly seen.

If it was speech that was being painted it would also be body language, eye contact, the mumbles and false starts, the repetitions of people as they talk.

But there's also what Bonnard was himself working with, and changing – the whole tradition of female bathers being observed by men. Bonnard domesticises it, makes it less erotic and more to do with mortality (aside from the astonishing colour effects, which of course can never be asides).

What Martha does – what her paintings do – is take that further.

The viewpoint is always from the bather herself, down at that level, with its awkwardnesses and the new perceptions. Skin tones out of focus, sharpened light on the little bottles, the slightly swirled hairs of her unshaven legs beneath the water, the heightened glints of the taps' metal, and the wood and plastic softened. The distortion of all those blues.

How can you say these things?

Sometimes, there's a part-obscured man, not looming. He's frail but he's not a benign presence – I don't think he's a benign presence. He's identifiably me some of the time. At other times, it's impossible to say. But always, there's the mediation through the female figure whose head you never see.

On her own flesh she erased her own scars, but she painted in others.

Echoes of the bathtub mermaid, maybe. For years after a holiday we'd all had in Florida, she'd tease us by repeating 'I saw a sea-cow, I saw a sea-cow!' This was a long time before she started on the paintings – the kids were only little, then. We'd been very keen on the manatees over there, which the first Europeans took to be mermaids. We'd all seen one in captivity, but when we were on a trip out among the mangroves, she caught a glimpse of a wild one. No one else saw it – they only surface for a few seconds – and the kids couldn't believe they'd missed the animal.

'I saw a sea-cow, I saw a sea-cow!'

She neither wanted to deny the importance of feminism nor accept what she saw as its outlandishly evolved edges – folksy new age earth motherism on the one hand, and aggressive anti-man-ism on the other. Not that they are mutually exclusive positions. She was certainly depressed by the channelling of feminist ideas into mere conspicuous consumption. But of course she was a hedonist herself – I guess most artists are in some sense *bon viveurs* – sensualists – but that's not exactly what she had in mind as regards the Women's Republic of Shopping.

Obviously, having the children was a bigger gamble than she knew. Children can't help but dissipate the energy of their parents, and in families like ours, most families, of the mother in particular. Her diary certainly suggests she enjoyed being solitary more than she enjoyed painting.

I once asked her what she thought I'd learned from her *as a woman*, meaning what she could see in my work. She said: 'You don't find the perfume counter in the aisle for feminine hygiene.'

A Renfrewshire Babycom

A front room: a TV, sofa and two armchairs. The TV is tuned to the Poetry Channel, which displays professionally produced adverts and five-minute-films recorded by people outside the broadcasting business. A baby monitor is plugged into a wall socket, from which can be heard various sounds. These include atmospheric recordings taken on the banks of the River Gryffe at strategic intervals from its source to its confluence with the River Cart and on to the River Clyde; interviews with the drivers of green tractors and of blue tractors; and voices reciting, in a less than hymn-like manner, the names of: the pets of the American military families once billeted in the west of the county; the typewriters manufactured by IBM at Greenock, before the invention of personal computers; the oil rigs used for the names of roads, crescents and avenues on a housing estate near Crosslee; the ghost railway stations of Renfrewshire; the cars made at the Linwood car plant, excluding 'Avenger'; the deconsecrated churches and the organisations now occupying them; all the flowering plants that grow through the security fence of the old Royal Ordnance Factory, Bishopton; the Brythonic monarchs of Strathclyde; the past shipyards of Port Glasgow; the soft fruit varieties cultivated in the walled garden of Craigends House, now demolished; the dates on which viewing conditions were ideal at Mirren Observatory; the first and last menu of the Hydro Hotel.

4

The Last Day

The whole house is asleep. Karen MacIlkenny gently closes the door of her mother's small blue car. Saturday: Stephen sleeps in till midday. Mum and Dad wake with the sound of reverse, but she shut the door softly. Precise breakfasts by the time she is parking the car on Observatory Brae.

No need for breakfast herself. A girl can hold out until tea break, a liking for currant buns right now. 'Like the elephants,' Gavin says.

She always cleans her teeth afterwards. In her handbag there's a sample-size toothpaste, a toothbrush that's soft, designed for children.

The bag fascinates James, so she tries to keep it out of

his reach. He secures her micromap of the London underground, a keepsake from a school trip. 'They've opened a new line since then!' – holding it above his head with his right hand, then grabbing a wooden clothes peg and a small roll of bandage with the left, singing 'Paramedic!'

Later, he says, 'Do you know where the word paraphernalia comes from? It means the belongings a woman can keep. Even after marriage.'

'A mine of information, you are.'

The bag has a strong card insert at the base, keeping its shape, and hiding two vacuum-packed condoms beneath. So far, mother-resistant. James, discovering them, squeezes the leather to see in, but says nothing, sets the bag down again, all contents intact.

She slows the car almost to a standstill at the foot of Highwood Road. The steep lane narrows here to a junction that's also a blind hairpin turn. You have to be careful not to meet another vehicle head on. Just as she pulls out, sure enough near-fatality, a large grey car swings into view, accelerating towards her. She brakes, and the car passes a breath away from her wing mirror.

Alan Ford, the brother of one of James's friends. Elder brother. A friend of Frank Chisholm.

He gives her a little thank you wave, as if she'd seen him all along and was waiting for him to pass.

Alan's father's car. James told her the last vehicle Alan

owned ended up a wreck on the back road to Kilellan. Not because Alan had been more drunk than he had ever been in his life, not because he was driving at approximately two point five times the speed limit. The reason Alan crashed the car, James explained, was because the car was a left-hand drive, adding, 'The visibility of continental cars on British roads is less than the optimum.'

She moves off towards the old railway bridge (cycle path, must race James along there sometime), but has to give way at the junction into Main Street. Roadworks with temporary traffic lights are slowing down all through-traffic. A car passes with an inflatable dinghy bound to its roof, towing a caravan. More holiday traffic trails behind it, the whole line coming to a stop. One driver in a car with spoilers and sculpted wheel arches starts beeping his horn.

Psychology classes. The first indications are boys emphasise speed when they play with toy cars, girls want conversation between the drivers.

Maybe yes, maybe no: she likes Japanese convertibles, copycats of the English sportsters of twenty years ago. Copycats that work, this time around.

She wants to specialise in adult behaviour, in aberrant behaviour, in phobias and obsessions – and the uni's found her a year's placement with the Ministry of Defence. A kind of claustrophobia, too secret for London to say more.

The traffic is still static. If the car with rally pretensions would let her through she could escape, but the driver isn't looking her way. At least he's stopped using his horn.

She's worrying about the time now.

The Ministry starts in six weeks, and if Stephen gets his job they could rent a flat together. He's 'too-clever-by-half' in front of Mum and Dad, but good company without them. Someone to be there, though you can't take scare stories about London seriously. (Except Caroline, the daughter of one of Dad's fishing friends: she'd flitted down from Kilellan and had been missing for weeks. Missing by choice?)

James didn't think he could take a year out and join her: 'You cannae do that with a computing science degree.' That drags a concession out of Stephen: 'I'll think about it, OK?'

Two motorbikes with laden panniers zoom up past the fretting cars and take poll position, just in front of the lights. Rally Man holds up his hands, a protest before an imaginary audience. Karen realises she's tense: she's certainly going to be late.

It's her last day: a summer job she's had for a couple of years. She's not doing the full stint this time, so she and James can have a holiday before the Ministry. They can't agree on where they should go: he wants Holland or even Belgium ('I am a Fleming!'), but a camping holiday in Argyll surely sounds more the thing: castles and stone circles and secret beaches. Mum likes James because she doesn't know him, so they can take her car.

Belgium? James's jokes and dictionary lore. Ungeneral knowledge, and a syndrome on the mild edge of the autistic spectrum.

Rally Man beeps again, as if anyone can do anything about the lights. But now he's seen her waiting: he reverses rapidly, dangerously close to the motorhome behind him, and she can cross in front. He waves her through as if performing an act of chivalry. She smiles a hostile smile.

'I haven't written your reference, yet, you know,' Gavin says.

'Honestly, it was the traffic.'

Her first task is tidying the shelves. Household pets. You couldn't expect psychometric matching in a summer job.

The spine of a book catches her attention, Paul Gallico. Fiction shouldn't be in Pet's Corner, but the class mark is right.

She stops work, goes to look for Gavin, taking the book with her. After a brief check upstairs in the children's department (he's been rethinking the Young Adult section), she finds him downstairs after all, in the staffroom. He's busy with audio-visual equipment.

'Sorry to bother you Gavin, but I thought you'd like to see something that's catalogued wrongly.' She knows too late this is Goody-two-shoes. 'I found it on the pet shelves.'

Gavin looks up from the back of the video he's trying to connect to a TV. He glances at the book in Karen's hand, tuts and blinks heavily, once.

He stands up.

'Karen,' he says, 'this might be your last day, and you might be a psychology student with a brilliant career etcetera ahead of you, no doubt in the Big Smoke, where all the really clever people live, but the librarians here did go to university just like you and one of the very sophisticated things they used to teach students in those days – it must've been an honours class for this level of intelligence – was the difference between a novel about cats and *a pet manual*. Now, will you put that book back where you found it, and go and see if you can do something of even moderate use before the public come in and start presenting you with really big challenges.'

The Silent Miaow.

She opens the book and there's the sub-title: *A manual for kittens, strays and homeless cats, translated from the feline.*

Carol says not to worry, Gavin's going through a divorce, and there are two children in the middle of it.

By tea break, he's in a better mood. He's volunteered to bring back the bag of cakes from the baker's, and he's saying he'll take no money off anyone.

'You're all going to need your pennies,' he tells them, 'because you'll be phoning in big donations tonight.'

Shirley tells Karen later that Gavin actually had a ticket for Live Aid, but 'typical Management, they wouldnae let him take the day off.' That's why he was in such a foul mood this morning. She says, '"A rota's a rota," is what I heard they telt Gavin. Mind you, he's no as young as he used to be. Maybe he'd no have enjoyed all that crush with all they teenyboppers.'

Karen perks up when Gavin makes his routine elephants-and-currant-bun joke.

Then he announces: 'I've rigged up the TV for the

concert this afternoon, so we can all use our breaks to see the event. The music might not be everybody's cup of tea, but I hope folk'll not mind the staffroom being taken over just this once. It is for a good cause. And there'll be a video a bit later on if anyone wants a memento. It's on Betamax, so the quality will be good and the recording should last forever.'

A loud drumming and whistling – from the street side of the building. So loud the Library's stone walls resonate. Everyone puts their cakes down – Karen takes a tissue out of her handbag and wipes her fingers and lips, at least her tongue can do some teeth-cleaning – and all the staff come out into the reading room.

They gather at the long windows looking out over Mirren's High Street. Some of the readers come up to see as well.

An Orange march.

Men and boys possess the street. Dressed in orange and black, they're marching beneath large banners, all the same super-saver colours. The drumming's so loud it makes Karen's body a tight drum, thump, and there are flutes leprechauns would covet.

Thump.

A drummer, as big as a bear, has a vast bass drum on his chest: he's pregnant, or he's a cuddly animal from a cartoon; he's beating his own foetus.

Thump.

The signs are indecipherable: the numbers on their banners look like food additive codes. The heraldry could be the badge of a fake dukedom or the coat of arms of the Wonderful Wizard of Oz. But the men hold on, twiddley-dee, thump, *thump*, to their signs as if pieces of painted cloth are more precious than their children (kids run in and out of the crush of pedestrians at the roadside).

Young boys in Rangers strips shadow the procession, a blue stream between the street and the pavement. Official lining-of-the-way and casual passers-by sharing a smug smile. Thump, *thump*, *thump*. Other pedestrians walking quickly away, faces down.

The march comes right up to the Library, twiddley-dee thumpety, *thump*, thumpety-thump, *thump*, thump, *thump*... and then they're slowing down until they're keeping time on the spot. 'Marching and going nowhere,' Karen says to herself. The flutes stop and the bass drums too, but the metallic snares hiss out. Tsss. All the marchers are facing the building now, Tsss, Tsss, Tsss, as if the Library is the target of their contempt.

The leader twirls a heavy silver rod in his hand, then hurls it high up into the air above him.

Tsss, Tsss, Tsss.

Though it's still spinning, he catches it with a triumphant snatch.

'He's handy with his sceptre, anyway!' Shirley says. She sounds impressed and lewd and apologetic all at once.

Tsss, Tsss, Tsss.

As she speaks, a boy not yet in his teens runs up on to some Council shrubbery, grabs a handful of small stones from the undergrowth. He throws them, one after another, towards the Library window. All fall short of the wall, but then he runs forward for the last throw and *crack*, the rock hits the glass.

Tsss, Tsss, *Tsss*.

It does no damage.

The parade's hypnosis is broken. Thump, thump, thump, twiddley-dee. The bass drums and flutes start up again and the march moves noisily on.

'That's why you went and fetched the cakes!' Karen hears Carol say to Gavin as staff and readers disperse. 'Were you protecting us, Mr Cutler?'

'Let's leave fantasy to Tolkien and C S Lewis, Mrs O'Donoghue,' he says, softly.

Karen takes the early lunch slot, at twelve, and usually eats her lunch on the benches near the Abbey. If it's raining, she walks right into the church and sits on one of the pews, surreptitiously nibbling away. She can see a huge Celtic cross that used to be on one of the hills near home, taken away for its own protection (weather and vandals). The Abbey has modern art as well and some of it is as fine as anything on that slab of stone.

Last Saturday, she's heading down that way and bumps into James and his friends. They're going up to Listen. She can put a name to John, Alan Ford's wee brother, quiet as usual (Alan inherited all the get-up-and-go in that family), and Frank, Frank Chisholm. He's quite a bit older than the other boys, and more Alan's friend than James's. She likes the look of big Frank Chisholm. A scientist like her, he's a technician at Radar and Gyroscope. He's got Alan's presence, but Frank isn't a car-crasher and he isn't a drunk.

'Are you going up for some good driving music?' she asks them all, but means Frank. She acknowledges James with a smile and a look. Frank answers first and they start talking between themselves: what are the best tracks for car journeys. They agree in ten seconds flat on Steppenwolf's *Born to be Wild*, and when she looks him in the face they both grin and she looks a bit longer. He has the bluest of eyes, but his hair is as black as a record.

After a few minutes James interrupts them: 'Well, see you tonight, Karen! We better not keep you from your work.' Karen takes the point: you can't flirt too much with your boyfriend in attendance. And she'd first heard *Born to be Wild* at James's.

She says goodbye to the boys, adding, for James's benefit, 'Bring me a present, then, as you're going shopping!'

When James sees her later he says he's forgotten all about her 'demand', 'And, anyway, Wants don't get.' In fact he's found her a second-hand Judy Collins record with *The Bells of Rhymney* on it. It's a hymn to the victims of an old mining disaster but it reminds her of *Oranges and Lemons*: 'When will you pay me? say the bells of Old Bailey.'

He doesn't show her the album until they drive up on the roads overlooking the Clyde. It's her suggestion they go up there. Even then, he waits. He parks in the empty car park of an 'official viewpoint' and they just look out over the dashboard across the Firth, towards eastern Argyll. She wonders if Frank Chisholm has ever been up here with a girl, but it's James she's beside. Both their seatbelts are still on. They're facing the hills and the water, the boats and the tiny lights out there – 'the greatest perspective in all Scotland' the noticeboard says.

James shakes his head, 'No, I'm not convinced. Looks awful uninteresting to me. Belgium still sounds more alluring than Argyll, if you want my opinion.' She says she wasn't sure she did want his opinion, and dummy-punches him.

A little later he's given her the LP, concealed on the back seat under his father's oilskin overcoat. She hasn't pursued the holiday question.

Today, she rushes back to the Library, eating her sandwiches as she walks. 'A gallus besom' Shirley would have called her, running up the Library steps, cramming the last of the chicken salad special into her mouth, glad to get out of the heat.

As she sits down with the early shift, Status Quo are on stage. They're granny's choice, really, so maybe working during Live Aid wasn't a disaster. Then the Style Council comes on, which is more like it, even if Shirley says the black singer is too pushy and backing singers should remember who they are.

James likes backing singers who can't remember who they are. He said backing singers had saved Bob Dylan's artistic career, even if the trade-off was Christianity. The Human League's *Don't You Want Me* was a work of genius because the woman answered Phil Oakey back. Pink Floyd, which he never played when they were together (cannabis camaraderie only, with his mates), had released a whole record sung by a backing singer. Transcendent, he'd called it, and Karen believed him.

At about quarter to one, the Boomtown Rats come on. She'd thought they split up ages ago. Yells, screams and hoots, and when the band plays *I Don't Like Mondays* it almost makes her cry. Bored children with guns, babies with flies in their eyes.

Shirley says, 'The things they allow in America.'

The desk is quiet in the afternoon. Does Frank work some Saturdays?

At afternoon break, Gavin has organised a lemon sponge cake with 'Good Luck Karen' iced on it in pink. There's sparkling wine as well.

He makes his speech while Sade is singing *Your Love is King*. He jokes about Karen coming from the countryside: electricity due for introduction any time, and you have to catch your own dinner out there. At the end he says he, for one, would miss her, and Shirley says she would, as well, hen. If she manages to escape back out of London, she's to come and give them a visit.

'Tell us your stories.'

Carol comes in as Run DMC are coming on stage and starting to rap. Gavin turns them down a little. She says the reading room is like a morgue this afternoon, and that's some phrase when you think about it today.

It's Karen's turn and she just says 'I'll never forget working here', mumble mumble. Then she has a bit more inspiration: only today she's seen her first Orange Parade. 'I'm afraid it's not something we uncivilised folk have, out in the sticks'.

She holds up the Gallico book she's got back off the shelf again and says she's also begun to understand the language of cats. 'So you see, in the Outlying Regions we can't *all* speak to the animals.'

She finishes with they've all been great to work with, 'Really great'.

After that, there's more wine. Sting comes on to play an acoustic set, but no one turns him up.

Finally, when they're about to go back to work, Gavin says, 'No, it's OK to stay here until closing time. I'll keep an eye on the desk, and you can all leave a few minutes before five if you want to.'

'If you want tae?' Shirley says.

Karen says her final farewells. Carol and Shirley give her hug, and then Gavin does. He hesitates, but then pecks her on the cheek anyway. He leans forward again and says, 'It's true what they say, Dumbo. Never judge a book by the cover.' Then he repeats what he's said in the staffroom, but it's more personal, 'I'll miss you, Karen.'

When she walks in, Stephen and her mother are watching the Irish band U2. The singer is in a cheek-to-cheek dance with a girl he's hauled up from the crowd. Electric guitar and the two figures moving across the edge of the stage.

'That's a Number One album for them as well,' Mum says.

This must be a game Stephen and Mum have been playing all afternoon.

Dad comes in and joins them in the lounge with a quiet 'Hello'.

Phil Collins is reckoned the greatest attention-grabber. With the slight help of Concorde he's bidding to make both concerts, London and Philadelphia. A world record. 'A supersonic gimmick is still a gimmick!' Stephen is saying.

But it's no bad thing to show off European technology in front of the Americans: they haven't invented everything. Frank would say the same. Radar and Gyroscope are a Scottish Success Story, no, they are.

James would have been better off a lexicographer.

'Heard anything about the job?' she asks Stephen.

'On the telephone table.'

'I take it from that, you got it?'

Silence.

It's no good; she goes out to the hall and reads the letter.

As suspected, a yes. The job title, 'A Customer Engineer', makes her smile. These techies: their language is at a parallel to everybody else's.

'Well done, big bro!'

'Thanks. I guess that means you and I won't be parting company just yet, worst luck.'

In Stephen-speak he was agreeing at last to rent a place with her. 'Well, someone's got to look after you down there,' she tells him.

Caroline's disappearance likely tipped the balance. Karen's father must have been the United Nations special negotiator.

'How was your last day?' Dad asks, speaking properly for the first time, and changing the subject.

The question reminds her to be somewhere else. She says 'Good', but she'd tell him more tomorrow. 'I'm already late for James.'

'Love's Young Dream!' her mother and father say at the same time, but she's already running upstairs to get changed.

The Beach Boys are just coming on, an interlude live from the States, and as she shuts the bathroom door behind her she hears Stephen complaining: 'A Greatest Hits in the offing, I bet you.'

'You're late!' James says to her. It's just after seven.

A video of David Bowie and Mick Jagger is playing. Tinny drums, after the parade this morning, and *Dancing in the Street* is bloodless.

She kisses him.

'You taste good!' – she's sitting down and snuggling in to him on the sofa. James's parents are on holiday, so the house is theirs. 'How come you managed to tear yourself away from the screen and declare yourself to the shower?'

'Judas Priest came on about half four, and I thought that was God saying don't forget psychologists need love, too.'

Is Frank a Catholic?

'That's the first time in hours they've actually put up the

phone numbers.'

'Are you going to phone in?'

'Let's watch this video by The Cars, first.'

She knows the Cars song, *Drive*. How's that woman going to survive if she goes on like this? She's drinking too much, taking drugs that aren't funny any more. Who could love her when she herself wishes she was dead? Who's going to drive her home?

But the film is a planet away from the lyric. It's footage of the thinnest of Ethiopian children. The boy is trying, again and again, again and again, slowly, slowly, just to stand up. His body is perished leather wrapped loosely around sticks. He's a starved animal the RSPCA confiscate and put down.

He is just trying to stand up.

Phone numbers finally appear on the screen. James goes out to dial.

They've both received their first credit cards in the last week. Junk mail whispers at the letterbox daily, promises, promises. Half her parents' lives were spent saving for things she can have with a swipe of plastic.

When James comes back she says she'll wait a while before trying. The presenters are saying they are having problems right now.

They settle down again to watch the rest of the concert.

Phil Collins has made it to Philadelphia, big deal, but she does like that song *Against All Odds*. You feel choked, no joke.

Through the evening they take it in turns to make cups of tea or fetch snacks from James's idiosyncratically stocked fridge.

'Avocados are good for you!' he says, 'even if the word is Nahuatl for bollocks.'

Carol and Shirley will be enjoying this: yesteryear incorporated: The Who, Santana, Elton John. 'Punk never happened, obviously,' James is saying, but maybe Steppenwolf will be on the bill: Frank's face as they strode on to the stage!

When Kiki Dee joins Elton John it's one of her Dad's favourites, *Don't Go Breaking My Heart.* He's got it on a compilation he keeps in his car. Karen says to James, 'I bet Shirley Paterson's saying right now, "You're barking up the wrong tree there, Kiki!".'

Just before ten, Paul McCartney comes on and plays *Let it Be.* Despite the hot weather there's been a shower moments before. The microphone keeps cutting out.

A grown man like McCartney and Mother Superior: maybe she's just a dream figure from primary school days. Nuns might help infants, but anybody else? Thank God Dad told Father Declan, 'a comprehensive education is more appropriate for the teenage years.'

'Oh, that reminds me – I bought you something a while ago.' James goes over to his father's bureau, drops the front board down, and brings out a single.

'What Listen doesn't have, Woolworth's can usually supply! I thought you might like it as a pre-holiday souvenir. An 'avenir'?'

He sits back down with her.

It's McCartney's *Mull of Kintyre*.

'I guess it's lucky you don't have much knowledge of the Belgian music scene!' She kisses him. Argyll it was.

James looks about to contradict her on the Low Countries, but they're both distracted by the start of the British finale, *Do They Know It's Christmas?*

A hot midsummer evening and a Christmas record about famine.

She draws herself away from him and goes to phone in her donation.

She comes back straight away, 'I've forgotten my handbag!'

'No problem,' James says breezily, 'I can use my Visa again. You can pay me back later. I just hope no one needs an emergency pegging tonight.'

He asks her how much she wants to donate, and then disappears to make the call.

When he comes back, she's turned the volume down to a murmur.

'That's the British stuff over!' she says. 'Actually, I think I'll nip back and fetch my handbag anyway.'

He is saying nothing. His face is as blank as he can make it.

At the doorstep, he lets her go with only a 'Hurry back!'

She knows she'll have to park away from the house, so she can creep in undetected.

As she's bringing the car to a halt, the grey saloon she'd seen that morning swings round behind her, overtaking, faster, closer than is safe. Alan Ford must be driving, and she can see the car is full of his friends. On her side, it's Frank. There are seven or eight men inside, almost too many for the axles to take. (In the daytime, the Orangemen own the streets, at night it's guys in cars.)

They must have seen her, but no one offers her as much as a gesture, not a wave of hello, not a look.

Two hundred yards down the road the aching vehicle turns left into a cul-de-sac, and the neighbourhood is quiet again.

She switches her lights off and unclicks the seatbelt. As she does so, she glimpses the strap of her handbag on the passenger side floor. She tugs at it and draws the whole bag from underneath the seat.

She empties its loose contents into her lap. She pauses for a moment but then holds the bag again, reaching down into it. She clutches the card base, and then she's using her two hands to tear it in half. She still has to prise the secret cargo from its hiding place.

For a minute, she sits there in the soft streetlight, just looking at it all, all her 'paraphernalia.'

The Cars' song comes back to her. Who's going to drive her home?

She returns everything to the shapeless handbag, starts the car, and drives herself the last few yards to her parents' house.

Just right

When they first met, Frank Chisholm thought Angela McCowan was just right.

That was the phrase he used when he first talked about her among his friends at Radar and Gyroscope: 'Angela – she's just right!'

'Who is *she*? Goldilocks!' Greg Carter said – 'Not too hot, not too cold... *Just right!*'

Very funny. Frank Chisholm laughed along with everyone else, but he did wonder sometimes how the lads all managed to be so quick with their wee jokes. Especially Greg Carter, who was only a trainee a year ago. Frank was a senior technician after all.

You couldn't say anything against Angela. You could only say things in her favour. She was 'just right' because, for one thing, she was the most graceful creature you'd ever hope to meet. Graceful: she was like an E-type Jaguar or those shy deer Frank sometimes saw when he went fishing.

She was a quiet, firm speaker, but not surly. She was good in all kinds of company – she was the kind who'd say the right things to the Managing Director at the Christmas party and the right things with your pals. But no one could say she was a flirt – except that is when she was with Frank, flirting with Frank. And she was a good looker of course – not one of those skinnymalinxes you saw so much of nowadays, but a real woman with a bit of flesh on her bones. She had glorious curly hair: light brown and near-golden in glints here and there. Her curls practically formed dreadlocks, and Angela said she must have had African ancestors. 'Everyone has,' Frank said.

So Greg Carter was correct in a way. Angela was a Goldilocks, but not the kind who had anything to do with the Three Bears. Some joker, Greg Carter.

Occasionally she wore her hair with a single neat clasp that straightened it out under all that pressure and kept those curls out of her face. You could see her slate-blue eyes properly then. And if she turned for whatever reason or you found yourself behind her, you could see the delicate wisps she'd missed, straggling in their soft corkscrew way down at the nape because she hadn't got anyone to help her.

'Not that that mattered!' Frank thought. He thought

those wisps were just right, too.

Her clothes sense was for the classics – not just cleanly cut dresses and skirts, she did wear a trouser suit now and then – but nothing frilly and nothing too casual; and nothing trashy, not on your life.

She worked in the jeweller's on the High Street, between the Library and Bags & Rags. They had met when Frank had been taking his mother's watch in for repairs. It had been a busy time at Radar and Gyroscope so he hadn't felt he could have a proper look at the watch himself. 'You could say my mother introduced us!'

Though Angela simply passed the watch on to Mr Cruickshank, who mended the watches in one of the rooms behind the salesroom, Frank would soon joke that his Mum was the matchmaker in his family, but Angela was the watchmaker. See, he thought, Greg Carter isn't the only man in Radar and Gyroscope with a sense of humour. Angela blushed a little at the word 'family'.

At first, they'd go for dinner and a drink on Friday night at the River Hotel – not the Cotton Bale. Franks' pals were good lads, of course, but you didn't want company when you were on a date, and the Bale had seen better days. Maybe drinks with the boys was just a phase you had to grow out of, it wasn't really a question of being henpecked. Frank would still go in for a jar down the Bale now and then, but he was maybe phasing it out.

He soon thought of Angela as his girlfriend, and, once, when they bumped into Mr and Mrs Cruickshank at the carvery, she introduced him as 'my boyfriend'.

A big change came when Angela passed her driving test. Her parents bought her a swanky new Italian sports car and then she and Frank felt they could go on daytrips on their Saturdays off. He could drive already – he had his own Ford Capri in fact – but they had never thought of going anywhere special together before Angela had owned her own wheels. Before she held a licence he had taken her out quite a few times, up to Inchinnan Industrial Estate – 'But *not* near Radar and Gyroscope!' – so she could get some practice.

'To be honest, she's already a better driver than me,' he told the lads after the second or third session. 'I'm only going for legal reasons.'

Greg Carter was at a meeting with the Production Manager so he couldn't make one of his wisecracks. Which was just as well as he was becoming far too big for his boots and Frank meant business with Angela McCowan, she was no laughing matter.

Maybe the Production Manager was giving the smart alec a right carpeting just as Frank was speaking. He had certainly been spending a lot of time in the Production Manager's office lately. The Manager seemed to keep him waiting for hours, before coming in and shouting at him. It couldn't be long before he was sent packing. You had to feel sorry for him, but he really was difficult to get on with, and heaven knows what stupid mistake he'd made to get all that grief.

The best trips with Angela had been to Edinburgh and to Glen Trool in Galloway.

In Edinburgh they'd enjoyed themselves that much with the paintings and the key ring shops and the ladies shopping (which Frank didn't dislike as much as he thought he was going to) that they thought they better finish the day off properly. They thought they'd do a quick walk around the base of the Castle. But it was a great trek through Princes Street Gardens and round to the Grassmarket, along to the Pleasance, and then up, along and over the Royal Mile, and finally down the Mound and back into the Gardens. It took much longer than they thought, and they had not realised that their car park closed at 6 pm.

When they got back to the small multistorey it was all locked up except for one exit, whose barrier was just being secured by a man who looked like a zoo keeper. Angela persuaded him to give them five minutes. She wasn't being flirtatious, but she knew how to say things. They ran back to the car, which was in the basement level.

When they were both sat down in Angela's red two-door, instead of starting the car pronto, she held up the keys for a few seconds, just out of reach of big Frank Chisholm's paws. She said, 'No kiss, no escape!'

Well, that was hardly a threat and Frank kissed her quickly but gently on the cheek. Not the first and not the last as he'd later say. He's always been proud of her.

'A proper kiss, now!' she said, all smiles – and so they sat winching in the car park for well beyond the five minutes they'd been allowed. But Angela knew the attendant was under her spell and there he was waiting for them, some quarter of an hour after she'd talked to him.

'Thanks, now,' is all he said, and made a kind of salute.

Angela said 'Thank you,' politely, through the rolled-down window. They didn't have electronic windows then.

Glen Trool was quite different. Frank for once took the initiative and said 'Let's take the Capri,' thinking there'd be many a twisty road down in Ayrshire and beyond. He was maybe wanting as well to enjoy the corners and show off a little in the road-handling department. It was the real sticks down there, not like Renfrewshire.

It was a longer drive than Frank had calculated – it was lucky he didn't plan day trips for a living, though he did work on calibration now and again – and Angela didn't travel well when she wasn't doing the driving. They stopped outside a newsagent and bought the only *Scotsman* newspaper left in the shop, so Angela could sit on it.

'The things they read in Ayrshire,' Angela said, and smiled a wee bit.

Normally, both Frank and Angela read the *Greenock Telegraph* and the *Glasgow Herald*, though Frank could see the advantages of a more compact paper like the *Daily Record*. That's what Greg Carter read, even though he'd been to university.

Angela soon felt better sitting on the newspaper and Frank said he had not been at all worried about his leather seat, but he was even less worried now. Although Angela didn't look embarrassed, he said 'Anyone can get car-sick. It's nothing to be ashamed of.'

They finally arrived at Glen Trool Country Park. The

weather was overcast and from the car park the whole plantation of conifers looked more grey than green. They had cagoules and waterproof leggings from Frank's fishing gear, so they didn't worry about the threat of rain and just got out into the forest. He liked the idea of Angela wearing his spare set of mannish waterproofs and she thought it was funny, too.

They walked along the trail for forty minutes or so and then turned off the path into the trees. The world beneath the canopy was a warm, dry world; sterile, despite the magical reddish brown tones of the trunks and spiky branches and the yellowy brown colours of the debris on the forest floor. Very little seemed to grow there except what Angela called the rational trees. They saw no animals, and almost no birds, so Frank felt lucky when a blackbird hen crossed in front of them near a firebreak. Her back was bent as she walked intently on but she knew what she was doing and paid them no attention.

They stopped just at the edge of a clearing so they had the advantage of the tree cover, as it had started to drizzle by then, but so they had a bit of light, too. Frank brought out some oatcakes and cheese and some chocolate.

'So this is what you get up to when you go fishing,' she said. 'Dressing up and snacking!'

'I do try and do *some* fishing as well.'

She had brought a half-bottle of wine – that was her surprise – though heaven knows where she could have bought it in those days. Frank had never seen them on sale, even in Glasgow.

It was very quiet and not at all cold – it was a mild wet summer day – and their picnic ended with a bit of horseplay with the chocolate and the cheese, and the horseplay ended with a big hug and slow enough kissing.

Frank noticed when they had tugged and teased all their weather gear off, and all the layers beneath, that Angela's waterproofs had not fitted tight enough to make any mark on her skin. His had, though. He had those reddish track-marks a nylon waistband can often make on the flesh.

As they lay in each others arms, now and then drops of diverted rain from the trees above fell on to their skin. She walked her fingers along his temporary scar. She said, 'This is the best nature trail in Glen Trool... but I still like wandering off the beaten track!'

The only mark on Angela's skin was the band around her wrist left by her watch. She always unstrapped her watch when they lay down together, even if she took off only the bare minimum because they were in a hurry.

It wasn't a lady's watch and it wasn't quite a man's watch – it was somewhere between in size, with a black face, a pentagonal casing and bold and jaunty golden numbers; there was no hand for seconds.

She said Mr Cruickshank had made it up for her from a couple of broken watches when she first started at the shop, not expecting the watch would last more than five minutes. She'd had it for over five years.

Angela drove on the way back from Glen Trool and seemed to enjoy making the Capri growl. Frank wondered if he was going to feel car-sick now, but as he said to the lads, 'I was too scared to feel sick!'

Greg Carter gave him a funny look at that, as if to say 'Indeed!' 'Indeed' was one of his words, even though he must have been five years younger than Frank. When he used it, you always felt like he was a clever clogs teacher and you were someone who never quite got the hang of things.

'I guess that's a university education for you,' Frank said to Angela.

'I guess it is, Frank,' she said back.

She'd not gone to university either, though they'd both been to technical college. 'But you don't need to take any lessons from the likes of Greg Carter.'

They stopped off at Girvan for some fish and chips and to stare out at Ailsa Craig from the harbourside.

'Ailsa Craig is all that's left of a vast volcano,' Frank said, 'just like Edinburgh where they used to have the palace and the parliament and the castle.'

'Will you marry me?' Angela said.

Choosing an engagement ring secretly could have been awkward, owing to there being only one jeweller on the High Street and that being Mr Cruickshank's. At first, Frank wanted the choice of ring to be a surprise. He wanted it to be a little different from the usual solitaire diamond affair on a sliver of gold, and he thought Angela would appreciate a bit of care about the choice. But he just could not get enough time off to go up to Paisley, never mind Glasgow, and buy something special.

They were working six days a week because Radar and

Gyroscope had a major contract on. It was a sublease from an American firm who were supplying the Israelis with air navigation equipment. That would have been good news if they weren't now so dependent on just this one order.

The contract had been given quite a lot of publicity on *Scotland Today* and in the newspapers. There were always two or three protestors at the entrance to the staff car park. They didn't shout much after the first few days but some of their placards said you were a murderer if you worked for Radar and Gyroscope. One banner had been put on the industrial estate's perimeter fence, near the entrance, and it said that Scotland was just a colony of America. Another one, on the other side of the road, said that Scotland was just a colony of England.

On top of all that, the company had been thrown into a panic when out of the blue, just before the contract had been signed, the Production Manager had resigned. No reason was given and the Managing Director had taken just one day to appoint his replacement. Frank couldn't understand how it had happened, but Greg Carter had got the job. Not that Frank felt he himself was management material, but honestly, Greg Carter wasn't much more than a trainee, university education or not.

Angela always said just the right thing.

'Don't you worry about Greg, and don't you worry about the ring.' She called the man 'Greg', without the surname, as if *she* had become the teacher, and Greg Carter was now the silly schoolboy.

'Actually,' she said, 'I'd like to choose the ring myself. I hope you don't mind. I promise I won't break the bank!'

Frank didn't mind that much. And of course the money wasn't the issue. He'd pay for whatever she wanted.

So one evening at Frank's flat, which was on a terraced street down by the newly-closed tanneries, Angela waved her left hand in front of him, showing off the ring. Though the colours were different, it was in a style not unlike her custom-made watch, with a small, light blue jewel on a silver pentagonal base, and with a bold, broad band of gold making the circuit around her finger.

'It's a present from Mr Cruickshank. Made to my own design!'

Frank wasn't sure about it, and this Mr Cruickshank seemed awful friendly. But no one could say it wasn't what she wanted. If Angela was happy, he was happy.

He saw very little of Greg Carter now. There was no natural place for the two to come across each other, since the Production boss kept himself to himself, and anyway managers tended not to mix with technicians at Radar and Gyroscope. It was a company that had been founded in the 1920s, under an earlier name, and though it developed cutting edge technology for the aeronautics industry – 'Cutting edge, Angela, cutting edge!' – it had old-fashioned divisions among its workforce. The technicians also saw very little of the folk on the shop floor.

Frank still had a drink just occasionally at the Cotton Bale but Greg Carter didn't seem to drop in anymore.

Frank guessed that the burgundy E-type Jaguar that had appeared in the car park not a week after the new appointment was none other than Greg Carter's, and the lads said it was.

'Racing green would have been a better choice,' Angela said.

They had decided to get married soon.

'I don't believe in religion,' Angela told Frank.

He said he didn't think he was very religious either.

'Let's do it in a registry office in Scotland's real capital. I'm Miss Scotland and you're my Mr Universe!'

'Glasgow?' he asked.

'You bet.'

He felt he was getting to know her way of thinking.

They had no family apart from Angela's parents and his mother, so there was no problem about accommodating everyone in the little registry room in the Martha Street offices. Mr and Mrs Cruickshank came along too, but Frank didn't want any folk from work.

It was a drizzly sort of day and after they'd exchanged rings – simple gold bands this time – they all stood out on the street. They kept close in to the wall of the dripping building, trying to avoid the drops while they were waiting for the photographer. Frank whispered in Angela's ear, 'Just like Glen Trool!'

'Martha!' Frank's mother said, looking at Angela. 'The patron saint of good housekeeping.'

'Mum!'

Frank actually blushed.

Angela just laughed, not in an unfriendly way. She'd had

her hair up in a clasp for the ceremony because Frank said he liked it that way, but she unclipped it then and the gold-tinged dreadlocks fell down to her shoulders.

Mr Cruickshank said, 'She's the bonniest lass on the watery planet.' Everyone thought this was a toast and spontaneous Hip-Hip-Hoorays were chanted.

'You're just right,' Frank said softly to Angela, and turned to them all. 'She's just right!'

The next thing was to have the official photos taken. The photographer had turned up by then, with an apology about a fox causing havoc on the Kingston Bridge. Mrs Cruickshank was fidgeting with her brooch – 'It's nipping me, Mr Cruickshank,' she said, which was a funny way to talk to her husband.

Just when they were all in the correct position, two protestors from the company picket line walked up to them. Somebody must have told them about the wedding. Both had a big bag of soot in their arms, but all they did in the end was chuck the bags at the feet of the newly-weds. It was as if the two – a man and a woman they were – had changed their minds at the last minute.

Angela's embroidered cream dress wasn't harmed but her off-white shoes were covered in the darkest of dust.

That was a bit of a shock for all concerned but as Frank said, 'Lucky they didn't touch my good suit – it's also my only suit!'

By the time the wedding party sat down for a slap-up meal in a hotel restaurant off George Square the protestors had become something special to remember the wedding by. Angela said it was fair enough. That couple must have felt the Israelis were dropping more than bags of soot at the feet of the Palestinians. Whatever you thought of the situation you had to agree that that was an opinion, and the sirloin steak was the best Frank's mother had ever tasted.

The honeymoon was in New York. Frank had had to keep the break down to five days rather than the seven they had wanted, because Radar and Gyroscope were under such pressure to meet the contract.

The honeymoon was in New York, but the luggage was sent to Tenerife, thanks to a mix-up at Glasgow Airport. That meant more ladies-shopping on Madison Avenue, and this time Frank wasn't complaining. It was funny, he said to her, how he didn't mind something a little trashy on the underwear front – straps and frills – though he didn't fancy women who looked too tarty on the outside. Not that he was actually against that either, as such.

New York was a fine place: it had cheaper records than Scottish record shops. Many of the paintings in the galleries looked like flash modern carpets or snippets from comics, and the waiters were very polite in the restaurants.

Frank had heard that grits was a great American meal, but the breakfast places didn't do it as standard. It's a Southern thing, the cook in one place told them, but he made it for them the following day. Frank said it was great, but it was actually a bit bland, like porridge.

When they got back, they moved into a new flat just behind the High Street, on land that had been a goods yard for the railway, before the line closed. Angela seemed to have quite a bit of money – she'd organised the purchase and only asked for a modest amount from Frank – so the place was pretty swish and very roomy.

It was a surprise to see Greg Carter's E-type Jaguar parked out on the street once in a while. He must live in one of these flats, too. It just showed you how up-and-coming a place this part of the village was.

Radar and Gyroscope were in trouble. There'd been a delegation from the States that had only meant to stay for a few days. Instead of that, one man from the group had been given a permanent desk in the Managing Director's office. He had been there ever since. He was to stay until the contract had been successfully completed.

Instead of lying low and getting on with the job in hand, Greg Carter was never in his office when you needed him. Frank had thought of some modifications that could save the firm a fortune, but Greg was never there to talk to, and he didn't keep to the appointments you made with his secretary. When you asked her where the boss was she always said Mr Carter was with the Managing Director and his advisor.

The situation went from bad to worse.

'He's really done it, this time,' Frank said to Angela late one night, when he'd just got in. 'The whole production line has had to be stopped because Carter ordered the boys to skimp on the platinum and the boxes have failed their certification. The Americans are sending a five-strong team overnight, and you can bet Carter's ass is gonna get kicked.' Frank did one of his American impersonations.

The next day, the Managing Director had been sacked and Greg Carter was acting in his place. He had the full backing of the newly arrived American team who were camped out in Carter's old office.

His first action as the boss of Radar and Gyroscope was to sack Frank Chisholm.

'I thought Greg might,' Angela said, when Frank told her the news. 'Good!'

'To be honest, I didn't like you working for Radar and Gyroscope. It's families against families. I've got you a job anyway. It's more than a job. Andrew Cruickshank is selling up the shop and he's selling it to me, at a knockdown price.'

Frank said later that this was him in what you might call a laugh slash cry situation.

There were several moments of high-pressure silence.

'Just like that!' he said, finally. 'And it's *Andrew* Cruickshank is it? And you thought *Greg* might give me the heave-ho, did you?'

'I have tried them,' Angela said, slowly, 'I don't deny it.'

'I've tried them, alright. And do you know what I found out?'

Frank gave a kind of wounded grunt. What was she talking about with that word 'tried'?

'Andrew is too cold, and Greg. Greg is too hot.'

Frank just looked at the jewelled ring on Angela's finger.

'But Frank Chisholm, he's just right,' she said, unbuckling her watch.

After a Wedding

The dancing at the Silver Lade Hotel was far from over but the newly-weds, Andrew and Georgie Urquhart, had said their goodbyes. A little earlier, Georgie had changed into her going-away clothes: a peach skirt and jacket with a simple white blouse and cream court shoes. Andrew was still wearing his dark suit with a sky-blue shirt and an Italian rose-and-yellow tie with a floral design. He had on the highly polished black shoes that he wore to work.

They were now standing waiting in the lobby, leaning against one of the long red walls.

Andrew's younger brother, Graham, was supposed to be

bringing their mother's car round from the family home just five minutes away, in the old tannery village of Bridge of Weir. He was going to take the couple on to another inn, a dozen miles away in Lochwinnoch. The idea was that the newly-weds would spend the night there before catching a flight to Florida the following day. A wet, miserable kind of snow had been falling for several hours, with a bitter wind behind it, so they were going to appreciate those American beaches.

Graham was late. Andrew and Georgie had been standing in the hall for nearly three-quarters of an hour. Occasionally one of the guests would drift out of the disco, letting the wedding talk and the music's vocals slip out of the swing doors for a moment and join the bass thud that was almost all that could be heard otherwise. One stray guest, Neil Galbraith, an old school friend of the groom, came up to them and said, 'I just wanted to say you're a great couple, a really smashin couple. Lovely. No I mean it.'

The other guests said much the same thing. Like Neil, some would then resume their original mission and head for the toilets. Others would simply return to the disco. Again, there'd be a second or two of chatter and urgent singing as the doors were momentarily pushed aside.

Andrew moved down the lobby into the hotel porch and looked through the glass door.

'He's taking his time!' he said, with a knowing smile.

'Ah, these intellectual types!' Georgie replied. Until recently she had worked as a nurse up at the Royal in Paisley. Andrew was a chemical engineer with a pharmaceutical company in the Northeast of England. Georgie was going to look for work in the Newcastle area once they got back from Florida.

They were still amused at the time Graham was taking to fetch the car, but maybe a little worried, too. Accidents could happen to the most sober of drivers and, since he didn't own his own car, he was hardly very experienced. He had been sticking to soft drinks all evening so he could drive as the responsible best man he thought he had better be. Earlier, Graham had toasted the bride and bridegroom with a glass of Irn Bru, promising that their marriage was 'Built in Scotland – fae Girders!'

'He's probably using the front-door key for the ignition!' Andrew said.

Graham was famous in the family for being good at passing exams, and not much else. He was in his final year of an English degree at the University of Glasgow.

At home you could only use him as a kind of underpowered labourer, but this was exactly what Andrew did. The two brothers had worked together on his many different cars over the years. Even though Andrew no longer stayed in the family home, the two still worked together during the holidays on do-it-yourself jobs around the house. The pattern was always the same: Andrew would see that something needed done in the first place, he'd read up about it, buy in all the materials, and then he'd slowly coax Graham into joining him on the task. All Graham usually did, when he finally agreed to help, was get cups of tea, hand Andrew his tools, or hold components in place while something was being measured or tightened.

Graham was always reluctant to begin work on a project, but always delighted to have helped complete it.

'She wouldn't start first time!' Graham shouted through the rolled-down window as he finally drove the old white Escort into the hotel car park. He drew up alongside the porch. Andrew and Georgie met each others look with a smile, and came out of the hotel, laden with their honeymoon bags. With a brief greeting, they moved round the back of the car to heave their luggage into the boot.

Graham got out of the car and just stood on the hotel step, under the porch's overhang. A thin-looking man, he nevertheless had a slight beer belly, so his suit seemed to both hang off him at the arms and legs, but pinch around the waist. He was like a scarecrow that had had its stuffing unevenly filled.

The passenger door opened and a woman of about twenty stepped out into the grey-brown slush. She was wearing a cream, classically cut blouse with fawn-coloured culottes – those baggy trousers that look like a skirt until they surprise you with a stride or a certain sitting position. The only items of winter wear she had were black leather ankle boots and a huge black fur-effect hat with ear mufflers attached. The hat not only covered her ears but curved down and round to conceal her cheeks.

'Need any help?' she asked.

Hearing this, Graham rushed up to the boot to assist as well.

But Andrew was quick to put them off. 'No, you're OK Linda...'

He effected a camp voice of hurt pride – 'Thanks, Gray, I've got it now!' – and they all sniggered, even Graham.

'You better get back in the car, it's freezing out here,' Graham said to Linda. He was trying to make up for being a bit thoughtless.

The wet snow hadn't stopped and the wind hadn't let up either. They were shivering.

'It's colder in there than it is out here,' she replied. 'This must be the only man who forbids having the heater on in blizzard conditions, and then rolls down his window for "fresh air".'

'It's Mum's car!' Graham bleated. 'There's no point in putting the heater on until the engine's warmed up. And it gets all steamed up if you don't have a window open.'

Andrew looked from one to the other.

'So,' he said, 'how long have you two been married?'

Of course, they weren't married at all. They had been going out with each other since First Year, longer than Andrew and Georgie had. If anyone asked them, they'd use a phrase that Linda had suggested would save them both embarrassment: 'Marriage isn't on the agenda at present.' She was a student of political science.

Linda was about to get back in the car, but paused at the last moment. She'd forgotten Andrew and Georgie. 'In you get,' she said, folding down her seat, and they stooped and stepped in.

There weren't any good roads between the Silver Lade Hotel and Lochwinnoch. The concept of 'back-roads' had little meaning, because only narrow, poorly-surfaced country lanes criss-crossed most of the county. You would have had to go halfway up to Glasgow before finding a half-decent A-road that could then take you, in a very roundabout way, back down to Lochwinnoch. Even Andrew, cautious to a fault at work and at play, thought that that was taking things too far. Cross-country it was.

As they turned out of the hotel car park on to the road, Andrew said to his brother: 'By the way, Mum got back OK, did she?'

'Yeah, no problems. The Wilsons were still there when we arrived in the cab, enjoying a dram. They kept us back for a while. Sorry. And she was fine when we left. In good spirits. She told me not to drive too fast as the car was camouflaged in the snow, being white! She'll be fine.'

The Wilsons, their mother's neighbours, had given her a lift back earlier that afternoon. She had not felt confident about driving her own car since the death of the boys' father in a road accident nearly two years before.

It took them twenty minutes to reach the first house beyond the Silver Lade, Kelly's Farm. Normally, it would have taken less than half that time to get there. Graham was forced to drive at walking pace, with the car moving along with the strange feel and sound of a near-frictionless ride. There was hardly any talk: the passengers were almost as anxious as their driver. He'd moved himself into a permanent lean forwards, arched over the steering wheel, peering into the way ahead, his nose all but touching the windscreen.

The snow had become colder and drier, thicker and faster.

The flakes were the size of gloves.

Although the heater in the car had started working, the labyrinth-shaped heating strip on the rear windscreen was not. To begin with, all Graham could see behind him was the faint flicker of his own brake light, reflecting crimson off the snow-ridden road behind him. Before long, snow had built up on the back window itself and he was driving with no rear view at all. The windscreen wipers were making a wheezing noise as they just coped with the viscous flakes.

'I don't think my licence covers driving an igloo,' Graham said.

'Don't worry, on a night like this, there won't be any policemen to check up on you,' his brother said.

'Reassuring, that,' Linda said, in a clipped tone. She had taken her hat off, finally. Her hair was a rich chestnut brown and cropped short.

In the sliding sweep of the headlights the large black and white dog at Kelly's Farm came into view, shivering in its gateside lean-to.

This was unusual behaviour. Its well-known routine was to rush out at any passer-by. Car owners felt threatened, cyclists terrified. Walkers soon lost their faith in the essential good nature of all Creation, and were only safe after sprinting beyond the hundred yards that marked the limits of the animal's self-ordained territory.

Tonight, despite the slow and unsteady pace of the car, the huge collie made no attempt even to bare its teeth. It seemed to be a different dog altogether. It looked zoo-bound, like a predator born into captivity many years ago, and displaying all the symptoms of the dark lethargic phase of clinical depression. The snow seemed to have made it a stranger to the potential of its own menace. Pursuit of the staggering car, the easiest of targets, was clearly inconceivable to the beast. It mustered a melancholy bark, and the white Escort passed on.

'I used to go out with Shelley Kelly,' Andrew said.

Linda turned round: 'That's a fine thought for a man on his wedding day!'

'Just ignore him,' Georgie said, undaunted. 'It's all wee boys' talk, and with all wee boys you never know what's true and what's fantasy.'

'What a dog!' Andrew said, with a tone that indicated he was talking mainly to Graham, and wholly about Shelley. Graham and Linda, as the self-appointed intellectuals in the car, looked self-dramatically disapproving, while Georgie elbowed her new husband.

'The dog, the dog! I was talking about the dog!'

There's a kind of laugh that involves you furrowing your brow, grinning, and pushing air out of your nose in a series of small anti-sniffs. Graham made that kind of laugh, and the windscreen in front of him misted up a little.

'Shelley Kelly. You wonder about the parents don't you?' he said. 'In my class we had an Adam Adams and, Linda, did you not say there was a Neil O'Neill in your Primary?'

'Aye. I used to go out with him, as it happens. If you "go out with someone" in Primary Five.'

'Not in my case,' Graham said, mock-bleakly, 'and that

includes High School. In fact, Uni was a bit of a surprise.'

'You were a bit of a surprise,' Linda said.

'Very *shaggy*, she was, though,' Andrew went on, as if savouring the earlier memory.

Elbow.

Anti-sniff.

'I was talking about the dog!'

Elbow.

Anti-sniff.

An hour or so after they set off, they had a puncture. It was probably caused by one of the many pot-holes along the way. The snow concealed the craters, but did not soften the jolt when the wheels bumped down into them. At a particularly juddering cavity, everyone else shouted 'Graham!' as if it was his fault. It was then the car suffered a puncture.

The two boys were now crouched outside, drawing their fingers slowly along the frozen metal underneath the car, feeling for the secure place where they could place the jack. Because of the wind, they had to speak loudly.

'Some guddling, this,' Graham shouted.

The snow had not let up, and they were shivering. Their fingers were burning with the cold and with the metal and the muck they had to touch.

After they had finished what they thought was a systematic search – without success – Andrew stopped to think.

'Wait a minute. There should be a diagram of the thing

in the manual.'

Graham looked at him in annoyed disbelief. Andrew wasn't infallible, then.

He tapped on Linda's window, which she wound down sharply, as if she had been waiting for some news.

'Can you pass me the manual? It's in the glove compartment.'

Sunglasses, a bag of change, a leaflet to Muirsheil Country Park, and a small collection of Marathon wrappers were removed, but the manual wasn't there.

'Oh, man. I took it out to check the tyre pressure this morning,' Graham finally confessed. 'I must have left it at the petrol station.'

Andrew would never have done that.

Graham rubbed his hand over his mouth as if judging how well he had shaved that morning. He met Andrew's eyes and then looked slightly to one side, at a nearby hedge of hawthorn. Its dark thorns here and there were piercing the patches of snow that rested on it.

After a pause, Andrew said to Linda: 'You better roll the window up again.'

She did so, with a martyred look.

Graham wanted to get them out of this mess. 'Can you not just put the jack anywhere that looks strong?' he said to his brother.

'No, it'll go straight through the metal if it's not at the right place, especially with this old crate.'

One of them was going to have to lie on his back and get under the car.

Graham thought that this was not really what Andrew should be doing on his wedding night, but Andrew wasn't confident that Graham would be able to identify the jack point properly.

'It's OK, I'll do it,' he said. 'I've had more practice.'

Apart from their suits, the boys had no protection from the weather. Andrew didn't fancy rolling around in the snow in clothes that had cost several hundred pounds.

He opened the boot and found a torch. Then he rummaged about in his honeymooon luggage for something he could lie on. He found a large orange beach towel, one with a huge cartoon tiger on it. It had been free with so many cereal packet coupons. Andrew and Georgie had changed their breakfast habits to take up the offer.

'Frosties to the rescue,' Andrew shouted, a little grimly, but with a friendly look at Graham.

Graham exaggerated Tony the Tiger's catchphrase with a teeth-chattering: 'They're Grrrrreat!'

Andrew brought the towel under control as it flapped in the wind. He bent down and flicked it like a tablecloth to spread it out. The Tiger's body and neck-tie were now beneath the car, and the Tiger's grinning face outside. Andrew sat down on the smile. Torch in hand, he eased himself under the chassis until his head had completely disappeared. His bright rose-and-yellow tie was still whipping around, even at ground level.

Linda and Georgie's faces were right up against the window, and every so often they'd wipe a little hole on the misted glass so they could see better. Linda had put her fake fur hat back on, and she looked now like a stern comedy gorilla. The women seemed to be shivering as much as Graham was.

'There she is. Jack please!'

Graham passed the jack, and Andrew started to crank the car up.

Work proceeded well after that, despite the weather.

Just as they had finished changing the wheel, the wind dropped and the snow began to peter out. They got back in the car.

'I think this husband of mine might just come in handy, you know,' Georgie said to Linda, and snuggled up to Andrew. 'For all the work ahead.'

'Another job well done – by your own, personal, boy scouts,' Andrew replied, giving her a wee hug.

Graham was glad to be included by that plural.

'Let's feel those working paws of yours,' Linda said, warmly, taking his hands in hers. 'Bwuhh! The things I do for charity!'

After a short while, Andrew said they'd better make a move.

'Don't you want a cup of tea, first?' Graham asked him.

'Aye, and a chocolate éclair.'

'Well, there's no éclairs... and the flask only has one cup,' Graham reached down and took a Thermos out from beneath his seat. 'But there's enough for all of us. We'll just have to take turns.'

'Are you a Boy Scout or a fairy godmother?' Linda asked him.

'I reserve my right to silence on that one,' he said, unscrewing the top.

Once they had cleared the rear window of its white layer and started off again, they made much better headway than before. The wind and snow seemed to have agreed a joke was a joke and had stopped altogether. A nearly full moon was putting in an appearance and they could see so much more now. Visibility was helped by the reflective qualities of the snow itself, lying on the moorland all about them. Everything beyond the car's own emitted colours – the delicate yellow of its headlamps, the lipstick red of the tiny lights whose reflection Graham could again now see in his rear mirror – everything beyond the car was soft white or had nuanced tones of grey.

'Even Kelly's dog would just lick you in this light,' he said. 'In fact, she'd probably just purr, the big pussycat.'

All Graham had to contend with now was the alien surface of the snow on the road. He had begun to get used to it, and they'd all relaxed as a new rhythm of confident driving had gradually taken over. He was no longer arched over the steering wheel, peering out towards the road ahead, and he seemed better able to judge where the pot-holes were and so avoid them.

'Dad would've been out in this tomorrow, eh, Andrew?' Graham said.

'Aye, he wouldn't have missed this opportunity. He'd have been checking his filters and his lenses for the big expedition right this minute, and he'd be blackmailing us into coming out with him!

'For a... *sense of scale*,' Graham started and Andrew joined in to finish.

'Which'd mean...' Andrew said.

'... *the royal blue duffels!*' they said together again.

It was now well past midnight – they had been on the road for over three hours – but at last Lochwinnoch was only a couple of miles away. They talked a little about the arrangements for the flight out tomorrow, and reassured themselves that Andrew and Georgie were going to be just fine. A long lie-in and a late late breakfast would put them back on the right track. Graham and Linda would surely manage to find a room at the hotel, too; a bench seat in the lounge bar, at worst. There was no question of returning home, now.

Five minutes ago Graham had seen the pulsing yellow lights of a council gritter some way in front of them. They were now following the lorry at a safe distance, the first vehicle to crunch its sprinkled salt.

He could see in his mirror that the newly-weds had fallen asleep in each other's arms.

He glanced across at Linda, but she did not meet his look.

She just gazed straight ahead.

'Watch where you're going,' she said.

Keeping the gritter's flashing lights at the same fixed distance, he drove steadily into Lochwinnoch.

Automatic Doors

In the time you were talking – in the time you were talking with her, with her there (here she is, was, you were talking together), you'd got back your hesitant mouth, the lisp, the mutter.

You have your old hesitant mouth with its thick tongue, with its mumbling lips. I'm like this if you like this?

She has everything, an everything – which already has limits; slows down as it speeds up. Soft solidarity, please please please (pleading and begging, directionless prayer your master).

Please don't let it be known, don't let it be known that this slur speaks the truth. 'I adore you / I hardly know you.'

An interview, as good as. Near-shimmer, and no judging eye contact. Her eyes. 'The most expressive part of the eyes is the flesh around the eyes.'

Cheekbones and nose scrunches. Some laughter lines.

You have hands that are just too big for you – all you can do (everythings and alls, in such a condition) is fold. Fold your arms. You're in a dream, years after school, wearing a nylon jumper.

Tuck those hands in.

You think maybe you can tick the boxes, Love Life, Good Sense of Humour?

'Love'.

Senses, and nothing sensible. Songs sing everythings and alls, nevers and nothings, in this condition.

Love does nothing by halves, but half the time it halves you.

Love's old-fashioned words, 'love' itself: in this condition, swimming with the throwbacks, back in heroic time, archaic, back in the body. You're childish as no child is; you're in that age of chivalry that happened never to happen, 'charming'. You're in the body's pre-prehistory, instinct.

The structure of love thinks it's against structures.

'In love'.

You're a body that can't be tolerated.

'Grow up!' they, you yourself, keep telling you.

Songs sing up and defend you.

No one can be in love with someone who's in crisis... Except someone in crisis.

You have got to get this system out of your system.

You're neither here nor there. Automatic doors won't open for a nothing like you.

You thought you were only suicidal, clinically depressed. Maybe there was something wrong with your inner ear. Doctors warn about self-diagnosers, but doctors drink too much and take no exercise. Trust me, they are friendly with insurance companies.

Fantasies of filmic suicides. Preoccupations with her voice at its edges. She executes her work with even aplomb.

Suicide and being in love: they're both out-of-category.

You're against civilisation as a by-product of being almost helpless.

Out-of-category: almost helpless, almost blameless. Helpless, blameless. In love, so totally out of it. Head over heels, out on a limb.

Dismemberment, and the infinite expansion of understatement.

You have got to get this system out of your system.

A desperate style, naturally, with absolute lacks and infinites. Fluent conversations idealised, empathy, tenderness. Desire.

You have got to get this system out of your system.

The Customer Engineer

'*Dr Zhivago?*'

'Uh-huh,' Lara said.

'The film or the book?'

She took MacIlkenny's clothy coat, pushing the elbows of a coat-hanger into the top of its sleeves. She nudged it into the rack and it slipped into single file between an old-fashioned anorak and a trench coat.

'The film. My mother was mad about the music. The balalaika!'

'It's a good film,' MacIlkenny said.

Split hot scones were melting their margarine on thin china plates on a camphor chest. Even in the snow scenes the television held the reflection of the lounge's tableside lamp: opaque mild orange. The MacIlkennies and their furniture populated the steppe.

She had said something else, 'Uh-huh', or had smiled a touch wider. 'Would you like to put this on.'

Not a question in the true sense. MacIlkenny stretched out his awkward arms awkwardly. The gown was being tied behind him and he was a surgeon or a mental patient.

'Thanks,' he said.

'Just walk through.'

'Through' meant arcs of hair on the floor and machines on heads. A girl was touching a man's downy ear, folding its top edge to place her scissors on the skin behind. Another was placing a square of cellophane on a papery-faced woman's setting curls. A boy was sweeping some of the fallen hair into the bottom lip of a dustpan.

Almost at the end of the room, Lara sat MacIlkenny down before a mirror. She organised his hair with a comb. 'Now,' she said, breathing out in an audible way, like a starting breath, or a breath that said 'Right' sympathetically. She finished her sentence: 'How would you like it?'

'Short, please. Short at the back and sort of thinned out on top. Just above the ears at the sides.'

'Lightened on top,' she said.

'Dyed? No, I don't want it *dyed*! Thinned I said, you know.'

He was almost chuckling.

'That *is* "lightened". That's the name for it.'

They understood each other. She asked him to go over and sit in one of the red leathery seats beside a row of china basins directly behind him. 'Here OK?' he said, beginning to sit down.

'That's fine.' She turned the water on as he lent his head back into the special porcelain V, like the roots of a tooth, holding his neck against the ceramic cool. 'Did you wash your hair today?' (Yes.) 'Is it greasy hair you have?' (Yes.) 'Would you like conditioner? (No thanks.)

After the first shock the water's temperature stabilised; it satisfied. Her fingers moved gently around the scalp, soothing where his hair and skin met. He could feel the froth unifying his hair as she worked the shampoo.

With his head back, the ceiling wasn't the ceiling. It was a small-gauge metal grid suspended as a light diffuser. The strip lights, trapezed from the real roof and hanging within the cage, closed his eyes for him.

They had been talking. 'Yes,' he said. 'Flexitime.'

It was four o'clock. Four-ish.

'The time the Company owes me.'

'I'm on lates, tonight,' she said. 'What do you do?'

'I'm a Customer Engineer.'

He placed the phrase into the air. After a pause he added, 'I look after sick computers.'

'I look after slick commuters,' she said.

He gave a breath of a laugh.

'Banks, insurance companies, brokers – they're all my

customers. I'm their "engineer".'

She returned the breath.

'Customer Engineer. It sounds like something out of science fiction. Are you on call night and day?'

She was rinsing his hair.

'My pager's in my coat. Some of our clients call me the Doctor, tongue-in-cheek like. They're only meant to call if something's very wrong.'

She moved his head up from the sink.

'Which there shouldn't be if the box was certpass when it left the warehouse. Usually it's the customer who's fouled up.'

He smiled as if he was embarrassed and though she couldn't now see his face.

She rub-dried the top of his nape, then lightly wrapped the towel around his head. 'Well Doctor, would you like to take a seat back through?'

'Right,' he said, adjusting the gown. They walked back and she directed him to a chair in front of a work surface and a wall mirror. He sat down. She unwrapped his makeshift turban and draped it on the back of a vacant chair a few metres away. Then she picked up a heavy piece of matt-black plastic. It was shaped like half a huge gasket. She placed it on his neck so that it touched his Adam's apple. It was like a sawn-off bib.

She began to cut. They didn't talk for some time.

He was with his little sister in the kitchen of a friend of their mother's. Karen, reading a TV listings magazine at the table, looked across to him now and then as the woman trimmed MacIlkenny's hair. Their hair was always cut dry.

'Would you like a piece of cake?' Lara asked him.

'Thanks very much.' He had not been offered anything to eat when he had been here before.

'Calum,' she said, interrupting the floor-sweeper. 'Would you mind making a cup of coffee and fetching a piece of cake?'

He didn't mind. He leant the broom against the wall. MacIlkenny was interrogated about milk and sugar, and Calum disappeared purposefully in the direction of the back of the salon.

MacIlkenny began to look at his reflection, the first time since he had sat down in front of the mirror. He always felt self-conscious when he was made to sit before his own mouth and eyes. His hair was slightly spiky now. Sometimes Lara pulled his hair with a jerk and instead of apologising just asked him to move his head in a particular direction.

'Do you programme the holes-in-the-walls, then?' she said.

He was surprised, as if she had butted in on a private conversation.

'I know people who do,' he recovered, 'but I'm not one of them. I sometimes deal with the computers that co-ordinate the cash machines, though.' Then he added: 'Why, are you after a handout?'

'Yes please, and while you're at it could you write off my overdraft! It's worth a haircut or seven.' They smiled at each other into the mirror.

'I don't think the firm would approve, but thanks for the offer. Do you often barter, or is it just the lure of filthy lucre?'

Before she could answer, Calum interrupted them with coffee and a small wedge of fruitcake.

'Thanks,' she said.

'Thanks,' he said. 'Is this the first instalment of special treatment? I've never had cake here before.'

In fact he had not had coffee either, though it had been offered by another hairdresser the last time he was here. He was slightly uneasy about all this hospitality. After all, restaurants were closed down for a single hair in a bowl of soup.

He took a quick sip of the coffee, and nibbled at the cake.

'We usually offer it now,' Lara said, as if answering his silent enquiry. '"We always seek to please, and are always looking for new ways to improve our surface." Service, I mean.'

'It's very fine cake.'

He took a second bite, and settled down again. He eased himself down in the seat, and she resumed snipping away.

MacIlkenny began to feel comfortable.

'I didn't want to wake you,' Lara said.

He usually caught himself dozing at the hairdressers, but not sleeping. His head would jerk down and always wake him up.

He had been deep asleep this time. He could feel the

mucus in his sinuses move as he raised his head up from its slump.

He had the feeling of having dreamt something of great interest, though he could not remember what...

'What do you think?' Lara asked him.

He focused towards the mirror again. He hardly needed to.

He was bald, absolutely bald.

His scalp had one or two spots, even a nick, and his eyes and forehead seemed emphasised. They gave him an intensity.

He was enthralled.

'I...' he said. 'I...'

'Halfway through I realised what would really suit you –'

'I...' he said.

He was the minimum expression. He was his white white skull and the dark lines of his brows and his nostrils and his lips.

'You needn't pay,' she said.

He wasn't fully hearing her. He began to stand up, at the same time rubbing his hands over his head, feeling in the contact of his scalp with the skin of his palms and his fingers that he was new.

'I'll fetch your coat.'

He began brushing off some cut hairs that remained on his skin. Then he began removing hairs from the cuffs of his shirt. He saw the hair on the floor. There wasn't as much as he would have thought. There were little smears of blood on his palms, and some of the hairs had stuck there.

She brought the coat.

'Thanks,' he said in a low tone. He exchanged the gown. He pushed his arms into the sleeves she offered him, feeling his hands through the cloth into the air.

'Thanks,' he said.

The Kids

A tank commander is ordering the charge in his pushchair on the towpath. It's autumn but the river is a snail's evidence, a weak line, silver-grey like poor solder.

On either side of the trickle, you can see airport trolleys that have suffered. There's a soggy buggy, there are fossils and fill. Quite far out, on the sediment right next to the water's dull remains, a plastic scabbard weighted with silt is lying not quite flat. It was grey and red the last time I looked, a different river. Kids precisely 1976: Gary saying, 'It's Celtic, or something,' then placing the sword and scabbard into the water.

The wheelchair down there must have been a veteran's, a veteran of the peace, cured, rusted-up beautiful, though two of its wheels still turn.

All circumferences are imperial measure, states someone's guide to a manual, but I don't hope for corrosion. I cherish the circle of metal that Shona Ash once accepted. Gold doesn't oxidise, for all practical purposes.

She said, 'This'll be you and me, will it?'

Ten years ago, no joy in Dublin with the morning-after pill.

'Sex is a sacrament, Miss Ash.'

'This place is a bloody theocracy!'

Fingers crossed on the queasy ferry.

Fingers crossed, the Agency will open the governing sluice, and the artisans, the grebe, will be back with the flood. There's always just two of them, out there in the centre, unsociable except with themselves.

Shona swims as well as they can. On a hot day walking to the Swan and Crown, she says, 'Hold my hold-all!' She strips to her black one-piece costume, steps on to the riverside decking and leaps. A dramatic arc, an almost frictionless plunge.

I put her clothes in the bag and have to walk across the bridge.

I meet her a few minutes later. She's dripping, but sunning herself on the wall in the beer garden. Soon she's glass in hand in the middle of a summer of women with drinks in their grip. The men have their football statistics and DIY – 'just knock that through and you've added fifty per cent to the price of the place' – and here and there there's aromatic cannabis. Most of the folk are wearing T-shirts that mimic sportswear. All around, the chatter from the workers from Oaksway Business Park burbles away. It's like a well-loved record you can enjoy turned way down, background music for talking with friends.

The men look our way, the show-off, but it's not just how you act, it's not just how you look. She talks as if she belongs to herself. Anyone would want to keep up with her, to be part of her solemnity and her banter, 'There's such art in the cinema's brickwork', 'The stately rhododendrons are taking over, all the way from Nepal', and the I-back-then can offer facts about the metaphoric fertility of standing debris, the economic history of bridges, how we're at the centre of Roman Britain, depot number one for olive oil amphorae the length and breadth of the country.

I'm secure to know Shona, as secure as any security. I don't think this. We're cheerfully alone with each other, Shona-and-I among the cheerful many, the exhilarating risk. (You're in confidence with your knowledge, the grace of all her body the open secret. You're a fine couple, said to yourself without sarcasm, smug doesn't cross your minds, there's no protection.)

The barge owners did not get their letters and the river was cut off. The level fell overnight and *The Sunrise, Maidenhead,* snapped her painter and lurched. She's sitting on her side on the river bed, and she's holed the elegant *Zanzibar* next to her. The *Eloise* has been scliffed down one side. They both bear their scars like animals in an old-fashioned circus: hurt in transit, unresentful, still willing to please. Even the shallow-bottomed barges look larger on the new dry land. The badly bruised timbers of the trawler in the middle of conversion show that its string of fenders was as useless as a daisy chain.

I like the shape of the old typewriters, their physical staircase of letters up to the mystical numbers and the quotation marks, ampersand and parentheses, but near the stern of the trawler it's a shallow-gradient machine from the first generation of word processors down there. Just the keyboard, escape and function keys the summit, next to seeding flies on some small dead thing, a crayfish now I've consulted the book, the armour and pale shears, one last spawning before winter.

Hard water and high oxygen content make a river habitable for animals wearing their skeletons over their bodies.

Accidents never happen.

'Look,' Shona says, 'the Pill comes in a childproof pack!'

Shona and I and children. All those years, impetuous or taking our own sweet time. Sweet time. Splits in the condom or calendar miscalculations – a few years on the Pill; three times, I think, Shona's confessed forgetfulness – all those years, looking back, you'd've had to expect a child by mistake. Everyone's read the manufacturer's packet. There are no absolute guarantees – once in a lifetime, a life.

But there are some teenagers who think it won't happen to them, and it doesn't.

'Here's to the power of the pink pound!'

We drink to Freddy and Colin at their back garden barbecue, somewhere without an Underground in Northeast London. We raise our glasses in solidarity, thinking, without thinking, we at least can keep our options open.

The slipway. A mallard, a fop in his green silk scarf, used to feast here on our thick-cut crusts. Before the crisis, he boasted more family success than we ever will. A week ago he was even confidently dressed down, plain brown in the moult of eclipse. Shona's mother would say he and his drab hen were nothing to look at. 'Shona's still got her looks. You've still got your looks.'

Undignified samples and keyhole surgery.

The agreement, finally, to stop. Shona saying, 'A strategic retreat, right?'

Mattress, carcasses and the skeletons of bicycles; a little beach of pale gravel concealed by the Thames before the emergency; collapsed waterplants suffocating themselves.

Then up on the High Street, I'm passing property agents, a pizza chain and empty offices. Hoardings around a gap site are promising more offices.

That's the building of the old Literary and Scientific Institution. Just before Victoria ascended to the throne, a local vicar stood in there before an audience of hundreds.

He told them, 'We need the citizenship of literature and the commonwealth of science.'

From here to Weybridge H G Wells's alien machines, part-crab, part-siege tower, marched in a line on London. A Surrey Revolution.

The Institution became a library for a while. It's now offices for an organisation devoted to fairgrounds. 'Swings and roundabouts,' Shona says when we walk past together.

The bridge is crawling with one-occupant cars – family jeeps and company cars – then the path leads down by the biscuit headquarters (offices, no biscuits), and that's you at the river again.

There are no fishermen with their military equipment now. After the offices, on the left, it's just blue gloss railings and the grey backs of the gas and water companies. On the right, it's nettles and alder and the stinking guts of the waterless river.

Down in the parched channel there are what must be two large fish, twitching, covered in grit.

Across on the other bank there's a large upright slab, the London Stone. It marks the last reach of the old tides, of the City of London's medieval jurisdiction. Tens of miles from the official city, this is the limit of the capital's old power.

The news said the pleasure boats weren't having trouble below Hampton, miles downstream. The presenter implied mass marvelling at the complex logistics of diverting the nation's water. London-the-capital-of-England must itself never see drought. The programme has a London backdrop: there must always be water under the bridges of the City, water lapping at the Houses of Parliament.

Twitch, twitch.

Lord Mayor, Prime Minister, here's your fish supper. Come and get it.

You hold each other in your arms and holding each other is always an act of consolation.

Shona and I, walking this path every spring, breath visible. We're wearing yellow all-weather clothing, brown and red walking boots, and there's a flask of strong organic tea in Shona's clip-buckle rucksack. We're kitted out, dressed up. We're colour co-ordinated. We've got the get-up that goes with get-up-and-go.

(Paintball at Adventure Forest, go-karting on the Isle of Dogs; we still enjoy a club now and again.)

This is the land of the Magna Carta, the beginning of the district of Runnymede.

As it says on the poster, *For the health of our soul and those of our ancestors and heirs, to the honour of God.*

My father, just north of Marbella, is worried about his own noble line, 'I'm so sorry, son. I never thought I'd never have a grandson. I can't imagine what you're going through.'

Pause.

'But I guess you can't have everything. That's one thing you learn in life, I'm afraid. Look at me, looking for work at my age. At least Gary has children. And they are such great kids. I'm glad you two at least live close to each other now.'

If the heir of an earl is underage and a ward, when he comes of age he shall have his inheritance without fine.

The Sovereign's greed and the aristocracy's inheritance insecurities: the English constitution in an acorn cup. It was signed on a marshy island fifteen minutes upstream, a millennium ago.

'Do the childless have a right to have children?' a dilemma programme was asking late last night. Shona had gone to bed.

Rights?

To no one will we sell, to no one deny or delay right or justice.

A line to prefer. Though you have to have a soft spot, too, for one of the more practical demands of the barons: to have all the weirs in England destroyed so that barges can use the rivers commercially. They must have known the waterways of the Continent, their grandeur and their wealth. They knew that law must make a state viable.

The motorway bridge would be a good target, the local paper advises, for terrorists. It prints a diagram to help position the bombs effectively. The only damage, so far, is local graffiti, by kids with no command of their implements.

When the construction workers were building the bridge's approach, over on the heath, they uncovered an ancient wooden henge. Heathrow itself is built on a ritual landscape, with processional routes and stone markers. Those monuments have more in common with the sculptural motorway overhead than with the scribbles on the bridge's concrete. All the graffiti are badly sprayed, sickly. They're neither organic nor angular; just red or just blue; they're near-words. Painted mumbles.

No one bides in the damp shadows.

Out on the other side, away from the boom and the rattle from the traffic overhead, the river now is just a stretch of distraught weed on the mud and gravel. It's almost clutterless towards the Lock Keeper Hotel and the lock.

We couldn't justify the cost of a reception at the five star Lock Keeper, but the Swan and Crown was fine. It was a simple walk from St Mary's to the inn: down Church Street with its conservation zone hygiene and converted brewery micro-flats, then across the bridge (sixteen bridal swans, as if by arrangement, graced the swollen river, as we walked in rough and ready procession), and then down the Hythe past the cottages claimed as Anne Boleyn's.

The Swan and Crown welcomes you with its creaking 3-D sign of a swan in sunglasses, though the shades are actually a crown that's slipped over the swan's eyes.

In their bridesmaid's orange flounces Gary's Anne and Emma were almost as well-dressed as Freddy and Colin, who wore lemon-coloured tailored suits and matching buttonholes (miniature gladioli). Alan Ford, one of Shona's cousins, wore a kilt that didn't suit him. Shona and I, in off-white and grey, finished the night with fashion's third prize.

The declaration of a wedding, the exchange of gold rings. There's so much rubbish that you gather up around you, within you, after a declaration, after a symbolic ceremony, but the declaration has been made and the ceremony has been enacted. They wait for you to come back to them; they wait for you to understand them.

The Hotel is quiet, the doors and ground floor windows boarded up. The aluminium chairs and dark green parasols have all been stacked together beneath a dusty tarpaulin that doesn't cover them properly.

There's no sign of the lock keeper himself, either, but above the lock there is water. There's not enough to reach the top of the overflow weir, but there's enough to call it the river.

Pitched across the path, a razor wire fence.

A sign admits the Crown Commissioners are responsible, 'in co-operation' with the Agency.

Two soldiers are standing behind the wire links. They're surprised to see me, but it's clear that my arrival breaks hours of boredom.

The younger one looks at his superior, as if seeking assent, and the older one nods.

The first soldier says, 'Sorry, sir. This stretch of the towpath has been closed. I'll have to ask you to turn back.'

Officials are always regretful, always speaking under a compulsion to do the thing at some point that they are nevertheless doing to you now. They ask you to do something by threatening to ask you to do it.

'How come the Queen has water and London has water, but there's no river in between?'

The soldiers are relaxed, but the more senior one takes over, saying quietly: 'Just turn around and walk back the way you came, sir. Runnymede is closed.'

If the military weren't blocking my way, a little further along the path I could expect a German shepherd dog to rise up against me, stretching its chain. It guards a cuckoo-clock holiday home for a frail elderly couple. If we have Gary's girls with us, they squeal at that point, and Emma is genuinely frightened I think.

More self-designed houses, boxy or over-elaborate, and then I'd reach the long simple hut of the rowing club. Finally, there'd be the fields of Runnymede itself, the large open park with its paddling pool and swings, and its great stretches of rough and ready meadowland. If this were the summer holidays there'd be masses of mums and dads with their kids, footie and frisbees, picnics and radios. It'd be almost empty today, even if it wasn't under martial law.

At the back, Magna Carta Island is an overgrown hermitage for a solitary heron. The girls always seem underwhelmed by the bird, though I love it if we manage to see him.

'Turn around, sir. You can't do any good standing there.'

Through the metal links I can see two grebes, fifty yards upstream. They've found space out in the centre, and are taking turns to dive and swim underwater. Closer to the banks, the river is crowded with other waterfowl. There are tens of ducks at the water's lowered edge. Many are birds that were tiny ducklings earlier in the year, now as lanky as teenagers. Flocks of irritable swans are raising themselves up against each other. Furthest away, there's a belligerent platoon of geese.

I shrug, turn round, and walk back.

Light Industrial

My sister met me at Euston Station at about half-four. The train had come in to one of the low-number platforms so I'd hauled my strapped suitcase and myself up off the ramp, past the Men's and into the main hall. Despite the crowd, that's where I saw Caroline, just coming in.

She was on shifts, she said, the next one starting in a few hours, and she was tired. She explained this with a kind of pride as if that was what London was all about. No hello.

I couldn't get a clear idea of what her job was. 'Light industrial,' she said with a smile. I didn't want to pursue it. I assumed something forgivably illegal. That was what

London was all about.

The concourse was packed with commuters, with a few backpackers and beggars here and there.

It was the middle of summer, but I couldn't help thinking of certain days in winter when our village's curling pond would freeze over. The pond was on the outskirts of Kilellan and when it lidded itself with ice you'd have a procession trudging down to it. First the kids and the angling fraternity and the common-or-garden walking types, but soon the adults proper would all come crowding on to the big oblong of ice, making it the top of a biscuit tin come alive. Festive: skating and sliding and slipping. They'd be enjoying the conservative colours, blacks and greys and browns, of their heavy winter clothing, with glints of a crimson scarf; hooded or balaclava'd, gloved or mittened ('fluff-warm' as my mother used to say). Together they created a tree-hemmed island of muffled hubbub, talking, shouting and squealing; an islet in a frosted sea half a mile from a shoreline of garden wall and metalled road.

Far more people were coming into the station than going out; they were streaming in.

The office workers' clothes were neat, well cut and well fitting. The men wore botanically exotic ties and some of the women were dressed in skirts short enough to suggest, to me at least, a new liberalism of the body. Though it seemed warm, I was the only one threatening sweat. Women in flamingo pink, in executive red, women even dressed in men's clothes, 'power dressing': the whole scene had more life in its palette than the tense Rembrandt shadows of the Scottish world I'd left at Glasgow Central.

The junk analysis was bravado. On one corner of the concourse the John Menzies was, I imagined, the last of definite Scotland before you were out into the forecourt. In fact, the piazza, if it can be called that, was surrounded on all sides by old-fashioned metallic offices and scruffy shops, some boarded-up: clearly a blood relation of every no-hope shopping arcade across the small towns of Renfrewshire.

I had no reason to think that the rest of London would be any different.

As we walked across the uneven paving, down towards the buses, I thanked God or whatever clench of good luck I pray to at moments like that. I actually said silent thanks for and to my sister, my wee big sister, meeting me here and practically taking me in.

She was a protector, a teacher, a sherpa – and in just a few seconds my mood had changed and I began to look enthusiastically on the frantic bus station in Euston's worn-out lap. I took the red of the red buses, almost coagulating on the hot tarmac, as a sign, not now of danger, but of brilliance, vitality, of splendour, an intimation that yes, things would be better here, or at least, they had that potential.

Our bus, true enough, was a bag of bones, metal and human. The advert cleanliness of the office workers was now nowhere to be seen. We were last on as the bus moved off, out of the station's pit stop, and I practically required crampons to get up the stairs with my case. We didn't manage to get the front seats, but Car stowed my luggage on her knees and let me into a window seat with her second secretive smile of the day.

I was such a child, and once on the Euston Road I just wanted to look and look. I hardly knew what to say anyway, and she was alright with that. It looked like she didn't want conversation too much herself, though she handed over her house keys, not copies, before she forgot, and said the names of places as we passed them 'to stand me in good stead'.

The first time I'd been in the city was with my father. He'd taken us both to the gates outside Buckingham Palace and to Hamleys. It had been in the days after my grandfather's funeral (Dad's mother and father had lived in a village in Kent). Because Car and I were to be spared the service, – we'd 'just run around and be noisy,' – the rest of the time was spent over-walking grandad's old and bewildered spaniel and playing with wood offcuts in gran's garden. Of the whole ten days we were in England it's the only one I remember in detail.

We were lucky and saw the Changing of the Guards. Dad said they were the set of soldiers that the Queen kept clean for visitors. When our interest, frankly, seemed to wane, Dad grandly, which is to say, as if casually, ordered a taxi to Regent Street. 'Taxis are for short journeys, trains for longer ones,' he advised us. Buses and the Underground he avoided, associating them with 'the British evil', queues. For someone whose company car was a Hillman Avenger, you'd have thought he would have been a wee bit less proud, and certainly not so impatient.

Immediately inside the toyshop the Queen's personal troops were back again. There was a huge red-uniformed soldier made out of Lego, black busby and brick-stepped eyebrows, and, standing shoulders next to him, his double in cuddly fur. As for the real toys (no one could imagine anyone actually *buying* those things), Dad seemed to be in an openly generous mood towards us and I was allowed to choose a hydroplane. Car chose a model of a motorbike, and Dad – I can't remember – though I do know he would have been unable to resist something concerned with traction engines.

Just before the castle of St Pancras, Caroline said, 'That's where the coach lets you off,' pointing to a sort of wasteland-cum-car-park, now the redbrick installation we know as the Royal English Library.

Beyond Kings Cross houses began to take over, homes above shops, but homes all the same, and then houses in terraces further divided into flats. The shops became the sort you can't quite believe are still in existence, that must be on the verge of closing down or, like Verloc's *librarie* or the genteel anarchists printing *The Torch* off Ossulston Street, masking themselves among ordinary houses, shops that must take their dinar or dollar from organisations of un-English activity.

For years, a hardware store in east London, in a scrap of the scrappy north-east end of the north East End, served as a Left Luggage for an Irish terrorist group, the Authentic Republican Irish Army (ARIA). Whenever the local operative went on holiday, Umbria as a rule, he would leave a few hundred pounds of Czech explosive there for safekeeping. You couldn't have that sort of thing just lying around the house.

It ended in tears when a bag of ready-mix plaster didn't stick to a wall. The police, the *Socialist Worker* said, as I read over someone's shoulder on the Tube, had to be diverted from back-up duties to swoop on the place: helicopters, the lot. This showed, a police spokesman recited, how much their resources were stretched. He added that most of their force had been otherwise engaged, assisting, to go back to the words of the SWP, a private militia make videos of middle class demonstrators on the site of a proposed motorway link.

As it happens this story was confirmed by one of *Crack*'s freelance graphic designers, an eyewitness who had bike-locked himself to one of the now-felled plane trees. To my great regret, it was one of many important stories we could not deal with in depth in the early days of *Crack*, when we were struggling to remedy so many of the news absences in the press. The shopkeeper was arrested but an unshaven photofit is all they got of the Irish para-military.

As the bus moved out of Islington's scaffolds I felt like a police photograph myself, aware of my mouth, the tired thin film of sweat on my nose and brow, my hair darker with a day's grease. Though it takes 72 hours before five o'clock shadow finds me, London and I both seemed like a word yet to emerge from its definition: unkempt, rough; in need of profound refreshment, mate. The many dirty small shops with steel grilles, some of the grey roller-slats already down – (it was not really closing time yet) – seemed entirely in keeping with the mood.

I realised, too, for all the brother-sister friendship we had, and I thought we did have that, for all the assumptions I had made that we did not need to talk, for all my pretensions to a kind of sibling telepathy, I had been, in short, unspeakingly self-absorbed.

As the bus moved out from a bus stop with a purple comb and an imploded old orange on the shelter's roof, I asked Car again, 'What do you mean, "Light industrial?"'

*

'We'll get off here.'

It was the last section of an elaborate one-way that ended in a triangular junction. When we'd clambered down off the bus, Car pointed beyond the traffic island, to the right.

'That stop is where you'll catch this one back into town and most of the others you'll want. If you don't get the right one, or if it's raining and you just take the first you can, stay on until Bethnal Green and jump on the Underground.'

My face must've looked as if it was physically recording the details, but I would need the same information more than once when we were inside. It was now clear I wasn't to pursue anything as superficial as how Caroline spent most of her time, but it was OK to ask about survival info. I accepted this.

We were on a pavement skirting a large housing estate, a kind of brown-brick multistorey car park for pedestrians. I assumed that we'd walk right past it.

Instead, when we reached the end of one limb of the scheme's enormous constricted horseshoe, Car cut across the dry patch of grass there, me a step or two behind her, always slower anyway, but with a luggage stagger now. Then we were on to the entrance paving and into the estate's central space. This, a planner's joke-quadrangle, was essentially for residential parking with a line of treeless wooden stakes in the middle, a cylinder of wire mesh hanging off them from staples. Though there were quite a few cars already parked there (shiftwork, I thought, rather than mummy's second car – seeing Car's life as part of a pattern), I was struck by the presence of two circus-coloured ice-cream vans, side-by-side but with different livery, and obviously resting at their owners' respective homes. For years, the location as secret as an elephant's graveyard, I'd finally found out where ice-cream vans returned to after selling cigarettes to children on other housing estates.

There were a few kids in the car park, boys of maybe ten or eleven years old, mostly black except for one who was Asian, just standing around and talking, boasting and laughing, slagging each other off in a way that was neither genial nor definitely unfriendly. A wobbly set of about three-quarter size goalposts, painted in cream on the brown wall of the wheelie-bin store, framed all but the tallest of them.

We were soon up some flaking stairs and into the

scheme itself. It had a deck arrangement, but the decks were quite narrow. There was not really enough room, and certainly not enough light for the original 'streets in the air' idea.

Much later, one of my first commissions at *Crack* was to get one of the so-called 'filthy London' novelists, James Ranganathan, to spend a week here. It had recently been renamed The Benn Community Village: media-bait, of course, but for all my leftist beliefs I couldn't resist it professionally, especially as the state's previous incarnation, a relic from the poll tax age, had been the Wat Tyler Estate. In Car's days it was just the Summerbank.

Ranganathan's first and, so far, only novel, *Mile End*, was trumpeted at the time by a number of agit-prop novelists whose books are now published as 'Modern Classics'. Then they were self-consciously up-and-coming. They also had reviewing spots in the daily press and TV and, given such a privileged position, would somewhat illogically cite *Mile End* as proof that the usual print and broadcasting media excluded genuinely original, raw-edged, anti-establishment writers. 'Sour grapes' the weekly and fortnightly supplements said, which did make me side with Ranganathan and, quite a few years later, made me think of him for the Benn Village feature. The extraordinary piece he did for *Crack* as well as *Mile End* itself (though I admire that perhaps more as a testament than as a polished artefact), are the only things he ever published.

I see that article as the start of *Crack*'s quiet but definite climb towards its now (I think) lofty reputation for incisive social journalism, from Ranganathan's searing classifications to the lyric humanity of the pieces we are running on Peckham and Camberwell.

On the third floor, having ducked into a close and up the stairs, me holding my breath until I realised the place was actually clean and pee-free, Car led me only a short way round the deck, stopping at a front door she asked me to open.

I jerk-remembered she'd given me the keys and, putting my suitcase down, began to look for them in my coat pockets. I had to separate them from their entanglement with Dad's spare set, which I now noticed for the first time, realising he would be carefully missing them. It also occurred to me how familiar the old keys would look to Car after all these years.

Instinctively I went to use the only key with a piece of sellotape wrapped round it. She nodded as our eyes met and I let us both in. If she was adamant I would not know where she worked, I was happy enough that this intimacy, her home, was to be shared openly. Never one to resist symbolism where others would see merely the mundane, that I was unlocking the door and entering first, I took as typical of her old if erratic generosity.

The door had opened only a third when I was stopped by something heavy but finely balanced.

I looked nervously at Car who was, all the same, smiling.

'Forgot about that,' she said, almost to herself, though also as if it was almost unbelievable that she should have.

A muscular motorbike stood in our way.

'How on earth did you get that up here?' I laughed,

squeezing my case in behind it and now taking in the scrapyard qualities of the front room. There were boxes of scraps of lino, all kinds of woodworking tools, spanners, screwdrivers, paint-dotted hi-fi bits, rolls of plastic sheeting, warped containers of undisclosed contents, and carcasses of pre-combustion mechanisms.

The bike itself looked in perfect working order, brand new in fact. It was surely not something she had been stripping or mending, though perhaps it could have arrived piece by piece – and this was the task gloriously just finished.

'It's a Honda,' she said, pointing significantly to a brave but tiny wing, the insignia on the petrol tank.

I peered over at the other side, and there was another winged badge there, too.

'Hi!' a voice said, and before I could get to grips with this Mystery No. 2 in my sister's life, a woman in a brown nurse's uniform came out of another room into ours. Her short jet-black hair was stylishly cut, quite out of keeping with her dull work clothes, and she smiled at me with no trace of professional standoffishness.

'You must be Wee Brother,' she said in an impression of a Scottish accent overlaid on what I thought was a Yorkshire one.

She gave me a kiss beneath my ear as I offered to shake her hand, and that was Holly.

She was out the door in a second though, 'Keep the bed warm for me!' she laughed, escaping, as I gaped, looking to Car for the low-down.

'You can sleep in Holly's bed, until we get this place

sorted out,' she said, drawing her eyes across the overflowing clutter in the crammed front room. Except for Caroline, the bike was the most self-contained thing in it. An offer of helping to tidy up was patently futile, the junk would have had to be tidied *into* something, something *else*, and a skip the size of a hangar was the only practical option.

'She'll get in just before breakfast time, and she's clean. Ish!'

'Fine,' I said, not wishing to look provincial, seeing a whole new facet of the city in the precision timing of mass complementary sleeping, and not a little disconcerted by Holly's casual caress.

I managed to add, 'And what's wrong with *your* bed?'

'Is that any question to ask your own sister!'

I resisted the mock-propriety, told in her best high Kilellan accent, a kind of Bearsden with added outrage; in Renfrewshire, businesswomen live and breathe it. It turned out, though, that on top of Car, so to speak, I'd've had to share her bed with yet Someone Else. Stack, 'a wood-be carpenter'. He was not on shifts.

'He'll be in any minute,' she said, adding, pointing to a mini-TV on an apple box, 'put that on if you want to go out. The pub we always go to is the Pembury, but most of them round here are OK.'

She grabbed the bike's handgrips, head-on like a lithe bull-jumper from Minoan Crete, pushed it back to clear the door then guided it out on to the deck outside. She picked up a helmet with traces of old stickers and made it a basket for some tippexed gauntlets and a ragged packet of extra strong mints. She shut the door with a 'bye' and a reassuring smile.

A few minutes later I heard her starting the bike in the car park below, revving efficiently once or twice, and then driving off.

*

I was not sure how to turn the telly on had I actually wanted to watch it, so I moved round the hardware-feeling flat looking for something snackish.

As I bit into my second, crisper, fig roll, secured from a packet left in the sink in the kitchenette, Stack clanked in with his tools (yet more tools!), several bottles of expensive lager, and some bags of tortilla-chips, 'to keep the wolf from the door.'

Stack, like everyone I had seen, like me, seemed tired, but I immediately sensed he was someone attuned to enjoy all states of consciousness to the full, including exhaustion.

He almost instantly had a benign familiarity so different from Car's tight-lipped affection. His casual explanations of himself and those in his life were straightaway like confidential anecdotes, and we settled down to the news (the on button identified), with proper food promised in a while from his own 'fair hands'. Stack liked sayings like that. In truth, his hands were muscular and coarse, with a number of his fingertips bashed to the colour black and one of his thumbs lacked a nail.

Despite this easiness about him, I got little out of him regarding Caroline's job-of-work.

'She loves that bike, though!' he said. 'Did she show you its wings?'

*

Both my father and I had known that Car was living in a house she had broken in to, but that could have meant anything. 'Squat' was literally a dirty word: it suggested most of all the preliminaries to the act of defecation.

To Dad, when we heard nothing for weeks, it meant worse than that. At dinner, almost like grace, he'd say 'She could be lying in a ditch for all we know.'

I corrected him, once: 'Gutter more like.' He could be joked out of his rituals, and by my standards that was a joke.

'Yes, you've got to look on the bright side!' he replied.

But he took the point. It was Car's life in the world of the city that we both feared, and I'm sure in moments of unguarded fear some premonition of her body laying in this or that alley appeared involuntarily.

I worried iconically, too. The picture of her in a countryside ditch was not a product in fact of ingrained pessimism, it was a diversionary tactic. Dad seemed to forget that he and Mum had both lived in and around London for many years, that *they* had coped, separately as well as together. If those two scaredy-cats could survive then the hard-nut Caroline had nothing to worry about.

I wasn't convinced by that argument either, but was willing to use it to get Dad off the subject and into his world of past splendours in the years just before and just after the War.

When finally Car did phone, his face was all relief, then

anger, and at last, once he got the idea that she had more or less 'settled', ironic resignation.

Car had been going on about the waste of vacant housing since she'd started going walkabout in her late teens. On one of her winter visits home she said she'd been particularly impressed by rows and rows of houses in the southwest of France, left, so she'd been told, by folk who hadn't returned after fleeing Vichy and the Germans. You could stay comfortably in places like that, apparently, and it wasn't as bad as the phrase 'sleeping rough' made it sound.

In London it wasn't private property that was the problem, anyway, she said, as Dad asked if the just-add-water nut roast was alright. It was the state of the council estates. Though the middlebrow comics had a soft spot for stories on the lines of, 'My Worst Holiday Nightmare: New Age Vandals Stole My House,' the Real Scandal was the poor maintenance of the council's housing stock, as well as, through their own incompetence as well as the poverty imposed on them, the boroughs' inability to build more homes.

'I'm doing Mr and Mrs *Daily Mail* a favour by occupying a postwar bombsite they'd never have the guts to do something about, though they use London's services every day of their life. Meanwhile they're tearing up the green belt with their skunky, barricaded Tudorbethan estates, all private gym and 'can I see your pass, sir'. Built like a cross between the Tower of London and Ann Hathaway's Bloody Cottage. And I see they're even bringing their poison penguin houses to Kilellan!'

For someone so keen on the welfare of mammals and

birds, I was struck by Car's acidic use of animal imagery. I decided, though, not to offer any practical criticism during what was a rare New Year's Day reunion. Dad had even conceded the preparation of a vegetarian dinner, after his own fashion, and everything passed off surprising well. He did not mention that he had already arranged to view one of the controversial new homes just as soon as the showhouse opened for business again, after the holidays.

I stayed long enough at the Summerbank to learn how to reconnect an electric meter without dropping the LEB a notice of re-connection, or, for that matter, dropping dead in the process.

Stack said that he first experimented with meter resurrection, *Blue Peter*-style, with the aid of simple kitchen foil. He'd had ambiguous success. He got a current, but only just escaped electrocution.

This, Car said, would have been Poetic Justice, as most of the chickens that end up in an Alcan sleeping bag have been murdered – she used the word 'murdered' – by being dipped in water with an electric current pulsing through it.

Stack agreed that proprietary fuse wire was worth the outlay.

I have never been tempted to apply Stack's science, nor to look too deeply into Caroline's knowledge of poetry (*poetic* justice?), or, for that matter, into her concept of right and wrong.

It was my sister who suggested I should start looking for a

place of my own.

At no time did Holly say or hint that she'd rather I moved out. Back then, she was an agency nurse for a very rich, very frail widower in South Kensington. He seemed to regard Holly with a dubious gratitude – '"Angels" is right, nurses are damn angels! Are you my angel?' – that would quickly and arbitrarily change to even more obvious contempt, 'Christ, I could do better on the NHS!'

'Sometimes I think my life's a *Carry On* film crossed with *An American Werewolf in London*!' she said one morning, as she slipped into our bed.

She found her job much more absurd than the living arrangements we shared, though she didn't regard 'our' life as 'ours', nor seem to cherish its magic as I did. In the few weeks before I started work, we'd occasionally go and see a matinée together, have a drink at the Pembury or whatever, but we were closest in those morning minutes of snoozy overlap.

I only risked intimacy once – an ill-judged kiss on the nape as she settled on her side of the bed. 'Don't spoil it,' she said softly into the pillow, and I turned away, embarrassed, disappointed, but unexpectedly consoled.

Not long after that, Car offered to take me flat hunting on the back of her bike. Within a week I'd moved out.

A Room Full of Botticellis

Fleming found himself in an Italian city of unrivalled masterpieces. He had allowed himself a day of sightseeing before his meeting with the Italian office.

As he queued in the city of unrivalled masterpieces to see the paintings of his beloved Sandro Botticelli, street hawkers had offered him watches, silk scarves, and prints of paintings by Botticelli. He did not buy any of their goods. One was selling wooden puppets in the likeness of Pinocchio. They came with a set of screw-in noses of different lengths, to correspond with the size of the lie Pinocchio was telling. In the city of unrivalled masterpieces, Fleming bought three likenesses of Pinocchio.

After two hours he entered a room full of the paintings of his beloved Sandro Botticelli.

That evening in a busy touristy restaurant, he missed Fiona Ballantyne. She had kissed him, and on her wrist had worn a purpley lick-and-stick tattoo in the shape of a ladybird.

He missed Julie. At the age of thirteen she was already investing in shares. She had a blue and white Snoopy badge which moved with the beat of her heart, and with the beat of his.

He missed Linda whose father had a smallholding and paid casual workers next to nothing for picking raspberries on it. She was Linda of no further than the nylon waistband. Her father had sold the field to make way for two bypasses. They were the airport link road and his own heart bypass.

In the busy touristy restaurant, the red wine was good.

He missed Helen who had a rubella limp that she blamed on a fall from a pony. When they were in their early teens, she had been infatuated by him. He had felt indifference, sometimes annoyance. Sometimes he had enjoyed engineering small acts of cruelty against her. New nicknames and teasing jokes were easy for him to make and he had concentrated on the task.

Her brother had thrown lit fireworks at him, but Fleming was on the school relay team. He had escaped unsinged.

He missed Helen. He missed her brother.

Fleming missed Karen. He had asked her to marry him on her eighteenth birthday. She had said no.

Later, she had betrayed him with a lab technician while on a student placement. She had been working at a Ministry of Defence unit devoted to submarine development.

He accepted gratefully the waitress's offer to top up his glass.

Fleming missed a number of women he had talked to at computing conferences.

Once, coming back from a seminar at Brunel University, he had fallen asleep in an underground carriage with a woman from Sunderland called Catriona. She was asleep, too. She had a coarse patchouli scent which did not suit her. She was working only part-time: she had a son who was nearly school age. Childcare costs meant her salary only covered her outgoings. During one of the conference's many coffee breaks, she said that she felt she was treading water, hoping either for a rescue helicopter to shine its lights down on to her or for her to feel somehow the gravelly shore beneath her feet. He missed her tonight.

The Italians have a great affection for children, but their cities are not easy for the under-fives. They are especially difficult for the disabled. Fleming's son Sam had to use a wheelchair. The city of unrivalled masterpieces, with its waspish traffic, narrow pavements and dearth of parks, would not have been pleasant for him. But it did have some pedestrian precincts, and at least one shop devoted to extruded plastic products manufactured under the Disney company's licence.

Fleming thought consciousness reached a plateau with the fourth glass. This was the fourth glass.

In the busy touristy restaurant he had enjoyed the pasta. The mussel sauce reminded him of the huge mussels he and Karen had swum out to, fixed like a rack of handbags on a buoy off Carrick Castle. They devoured the fleshy shellfish beside a campfire that evening.

It was the wine he was savouring tonight. The pound was strong in Europe and he could afford more expensive and more satisfying wines abroad. The waitress who had served him to begin with, and who had humoured his flirting, had had to go home suddenly, after receiving a message on her mobile phone. Earlier, she had said that this was the last night the busy touristy restaurant would be open for several weeks. New management would start refurbishment early tomorrow morning. She said that the new management was not a chain.

The wine she had chosen for him was both fragrant and light.

He missed his good friends. All his good friends were men. He silently thanked Danny and Patrick and Adam for all the films and paintings and novels they'd shared on their trips together, and for their boozy talk on the now scarce late night sessions. Fleming would have known little about paintings and novels if he hadn't met Danny fifteen years ago. He would have known nothing about football.

One night Danny had talked about Burns and Catullus as poets who wrote their own presents. After that, Fleming had started to read poetry. His favourites were Burns and

169

translations of Catullus, but he had started to read Virginia Woolf as if her novels were verse.

The new waitress showed him the dessert wine he had requested and she poured him a glass.

Fleming missed Anne and the children. He knew she did most of the physical work in the household, looking after Sam and now Chloe and Ken, perfect thank god. She organised things, which meant he took less responsibility for everything in the home. He knew he would never know Sam and Chloe and Ken in the way that Anne knew them already.

The children were spoilt. No room was safe in their house from the plunder of toy shops, and there were signs of chubbiness in Sam which only Anne's naturally slim figure suggested might in the future be kept in check. Fleming was aware that his children were spoilt and he was aware that they were getting fat, but he always brought something back for them from company trips. He brought toys made by multinational companies and he brought sweets made in the local region.

The best times that he had with his children were not those occasioned by gadgets with flashing lights and synthesised voices reciting letters of the alphabet. The best times that he had with his children were not those occasioned by Turkish delight and Swiss chocolates. But when he returned from abroad the children now looked forward to toys and to sweets.

The likenesses of Pinocchio were not made under the licence of a multinational company and they were not edible.

In a busy touristy restaurant in the city of unrivalled masterpieces, Fleming settled his bill. He drunkenly asked the current waitress to thank the first waitress for her kindness. He asked the current waitress to share the tip with the first waitress.

He walked a little unsteadily back to his hotel near the railway station.

As he came to the right street he heard someone say 'Quanto costo il blow job?'

He looked across the road and saw up ahead an English-speaking tourist talking fairly softly to an Italian woman, who was standing at the entrance to another hotel. He was an American, or perhaps a Canadian. In reply, she was counting in tens with her hands. They clearly enjoyed the language difficulties, and they agreed the price in a friendly way. Then they walked off together.

Fleming walked on until he reached his hotel.

As he entered the lobby, he realised he had forgotten something. He realised he had forgotten the three likenesses of Pinocchio. He had left them on an unoccupied chair in the busy touristy restaurant.

The busy touristy restaurant would be closed now, and it would be closed tomorrow, too, prior to refurbishment.

In the morning he could go back to the gallery and buy replacements for the likenesses of Pinocchio from the street trader. To do that, he would have to miss his meeting with the Italian office. He was in Italy solely for a meeting with the Italian office.

You cannot miss someone you have not met. You

cannot miss someone you have not met only a minute ago. In the city of unrivalled masterpieces Fleming missed the North American tourist and the woman who could count with her fingers.

Also available from 11:9

Blue Poppies 1-903238-55-2
Jonathan Falla
You'll be lucky to read a better novel this year   *Scotsman*

The Dark Ship 1-903238-57-9
Anne MacLeod
A fine, mature and moving book.   *Herald*

Dead Letter House 1-903238-29-3
Drew Campbell
The sour uncertainties of Pulp Fiction's spectacular bloodiness, the dreamlike mysteriousness of Kubrick's *Eyes Wide Shut*, the typographical experimentalism of a 40-years-younger Alasdair Gray crash around alongside moral self-questioning and tough optimism ... the pace, energy and drive of the nameless wanderer's nightmare is undeniable.   *Scotsman*

Delilah's 1-903238-54-4
John Maley
Writer of *Daddy's Girl*, winner of Grand Jury Prize, Cannes 2001.
Described as 'exquisite' by the *Daily Telegraph*.

The Gravy Star 1-903238-26-9
Hamish MacDonald
A moving and often funny portrait ... of the profound relationship between Glasgow and the wild land to its north.
James Robertson, author of *The Fanatic*

Glasgow Kiss 1-903238-26-9
Anthology of new writing from Glasgow
A remarkably varied and confident batch of tales.   Edwin Morgan

Hi Bonnybrig 1-903238-16-1
Shug Hanlan
Imagine Kurt Vonnegut after one too many vodka and Irn Brus and you're
halfway there.   *Sunday Herald*

Life Drawing 1-903238-13-7
Linda Cracknell
Life Drawing brilliantly illuminates the contradictions of its
narrator's self image ... Linda Cracknell brings female experience haunt-
ingly to life.   *Scotsman*

Occasional Demons 1-903238-12-9
Raymond Soltysek
a bruising collection ... Potent, seductive, darkly amusing tales that leave
you exhausted by their very intensity.   *Sunday Herald*

Rousseau Moon 1-903238-15-3
David Cameron
The most interesting and promising debut for many years. [The prose has]
a quality of verbal alchemy by which it transmutes the base matter of
common experience into something like gold.   *Scotsman*

Strange Faith 1-903238-28-5
Graeme Williamson
Williamson's lucid narrative is philosophically adept and intriguing – a
profound insight into changing states of identity and a search for personal freedom.   *Edinburgh Review*

The Tin Man 1-903238-11-0
Martin Shannon
Funny and heartfelt, Shannon's is an uncommonly authentic voice that
suggests an engaging new talent.   *Guardian*

The Wolfclaw Chronicles 1-903238-10-2
Tom Bryan
Tom Bryan's pedigree as a poet and all round littérateur shines through in
The Wolfclaw Chronicles – while reading this his first novel you constantly
sense a steady hand on the tiller ... a playful and empassioned novel.
                                                                  Scotsman

If you enjoyed this book, here is a selection of other titles from 11:9:

Blue Poppies	Jonathan Falla	£6.99 *
The Dark Ship	Anne MacLeod	£6.99/$15.00
Dead Letter House	Drew Campbell	£7.99/$13.95
Delilah's	John Maley	£9.99/$15.00
Glasgow Kiss (anthology)	new writers	£6.99/$13.95
The Gravy Star	Hamish MacDonald	£9.99/$15.00
Hi Bonnybrig	Shug Hanlan	£9.99/$15.00
Life Drawing	Linda Cracknell	£9.99/$15.00
Occasional Demons	Raymond Soltysek	£9.99/$15.00
Rousseau Moon	David Cameron	£9.99/$15.00
Strange Faith	Graeme Williamson	£9.99/$15.00
The Tin Man	Martin Shannon	£9.99/$15.00
The Wolfclaw Chronicles	Tom Bryan	£9.99/$15.00

11:9 books are available from bookshops or direct from www.nwp.sol.co.uk and www.11-9.co.uk. Alternatively, books can be ordered from the publisher POST FREE (UK ONLY). Just tick the titles you want and fill in the form below. Prices and availability subject to change without notice.

Overseas postal rates:
Postage and packing for overseas orders will be charged at 20% of total cost.
Please enclose a cheque/PO (£ or US$) made payable to Neil Wilson Publishing Ltd. T/A 11:9. Alternatively, payment can be made by credit card (Visa and Mastercard only, in £ Sterling).

Send your order to: Neil Wilson Publishing, 303a, The Pentagon Centre, 36 Washington Street, Glasgow, G3 8AZ. Orders can be sent post free anywhere in the UK as FREEPOST NWP.
E-mail address: info@nwp.sol.co.uk

Name:..

Address ....
....
....

If you would prefer to pay by credit card, please complete:
Please debit my Visa/Mastercard (delete as applicable).
card number:...
Start date: .... Expiry date:...................................
Signature:..

* Not available in USA.